I0663703

MASTERED

Book 1: The MASTERED Saga

K.L. Silver

Copyright © 2013 K.L. Silver

All rights reserved under international and Pan-American Copyright Conventions. No part of this publication may be used or reproduced in any manner whatsoever without the prior written permission of the publisher/author, except in the case of brief quotations embodied in reviews.

This is a work of fiction. Names, characters, places and incidents either are the product of the author's imagination or are used fictitiously. Any resemblance to actual persons, living or dead, events or locales is entirely coincidental.

ISBN: 9781928121046
Published by K.L. Silver
http://authorklsilver.com

Dedication

To my children: Marli, Matthew, Cassandra, Tiger and Roxanna. Whether they like it or not.

* * * * *

Acknowledgments

There is no 'I' in NOVEL. It takes a lot of support and technical know-how to so-called self-publish a book. I'm grateful for the fine folks that have held my hand and helped me up along the way.

Alexandra Lucas has been instrumental in so many ways, I can't begin to list them. It would fill a novel unto itself.

Nancy Pracht is my PA, heads up my street team, and makes me laugh(and cry) every day. This woman is ALWAYS up!

My beautiful Belles (Silver's Ballsy Belles) make up the ballsiest street team in town. I appreciate each and every one of you.

Dee and Ell are both creative, talented, and generous. I can't begin to thank you.

Last but not least, a special shout-out to Michael, a Ballsy Belle, a wonderful friend, and a great sounding board!

Chapter 1

She was late. *Again.*

Without a modicum of grace, Missy Weaver threw a pound of ground beef, an onion, and a container of lemonade into a re-usable bag at the checkout counter. After three consecutive ten hour workdays, she felt heavy with fatigue. She could easily pass as the poster child for 'disheveled mess'.

Nonetheless, the cupboard was bare, the hour was late, and her son would be starving.

Her mind, as usual, was skipping three steps ahead of her actions. The to-do list which defined her existence was a demanding taskmaster, indeed. On the up side, it left little time for troublesome pursuits such as soul-searching and introspection.

Grimacing in acknowledgement of this sad truth, Missy was distracted by two peculiar sensations. A shiver ran the length of her spine, culminating at her scalp. More disconcerting was the unmistakable heat of eyes boring into her. Missy began to feel like some rare and exotic butterfly pinned beneath a high-powered microscope.

There was no denying the irresistible curiosity that held her within its clutches. Her frenzied movements slowed, seemingly of their own accord. There was no alternative but to steal a glimpse of the man whose presence she sensed so strongly.

He was standing innocuously enough behind her, awaiting his turn in line. Yet, there was a mysterious slant to a dangerously sensual pair of lips. Try as she might, Missy could not tear her eyes from them. The intended stolen glimpse was now a full-fledged ogle.

A dizzying aura of competence and authority emanated from this man. For Missy, his proximity acted as a vacuum. It sucked the air from her lungs and the usual inhibitions from her behavior.

Time seemed to stand still right along with her. In slowed motion, she dragged her eyes upwards to his. Upon impact, everything tumbled into place. Comprehension dawned clear as a mountain morning. Apprehension came close on its heels, and was gaining ground fast.

He knows! The quiet yet perceptive intensity in his eyes caused the exact opposite effect in Missy. Her ears began to ring and her chest to heave. The only available course of action was to glance down before him.

"That'll be eight dollars, thirty-three cents. How are you paying?"

The strident voice of the impatient cashier brought her back. Back to the reality of her life which included a teenage son. At that very moment, Christopher was home, hungry, and awaiting his mother and his dinner. And, not necessarily in that order, considering the hour.

Missy's trembling fingers could not pay fast enough. She failed at disguising what could only be described as slack-jawed gawping. Blushing head to toe, she gathered groceries in one hand, purse in the other, and fled with what little dignity remained her.

Where's the car? Struggling to regain balance and bearings, she raced in what she hoped was the general direction. Confusion and clarity flooded her consciousness and battled for supremacy.

Confusion triumphed. Fragmented emotions ping-ponged through her body. Disjointed thoughts assaulted her brain.

While she had no idea who he was, she instinctively knew *what* he was. No matter that she wasn't able to assign it a word. She was flabbergasted at the sensation of her soul beckoning for him in that moment of suspended time. In truth, it had wantonly exposed itself for his perusal.

Indignant at the notion that she might expose anything for anyone, wantonly or otherwise, Missy focused on the benign. She rummaged through her purse for her car keys, intent on putting the bizarre encounter behind her. That is, until an unmistakable aura demolished her good intentions. Searching ceased. Resolution crumbled.

Long seconds ticked by before she was able to scoff at the antics of an overwrought imagination. Locating the keys, she dismissed her foolishness, along with an unexpected pang of regret.

He appeared then, stepping out from between the rows of parked cars. She knew she ought to be terrified. Common sense told her to run, to scream. At the very least, she should attempt to poke his eyes out with the car key. The sudden appearance of a strange man in a dimly lit parking lot rarely boded well. One heard of such tragedies more and more often, it seemed.

And yet, weak-kneed and goggle-eyed, she stood silent and immobile. Missy was the proverbial deer, paralyzed in the hypnotic headlights that were his eyes. Without a word, he gazed down at her—*into* her. She was powerless to look away.

Already, she had no choice...

Chapter 2

"Eyes down, little one." At last, after what seemed an eternity locked spellbound within his gaze, he spoke.

His voice was no less mesmerizing than his eyes. Although it wasn't possible, its resonance seemed oddly familiar to Missy. Deep and firm, it possessed the quiet non-urgency of a man used to being listened to. Used to being heard. And, most pertinent: used to being obeyed.

Without hesitation and with no trace of fear, that's what Missy did. She obeyed. Thoughts of time and work and dinner and stress diminished to the status of inconsequential. Lists took a distant back seat to this stranger who somehow wasn't a stranger.

She recognized this man on a cellular level deep within her soul. And, deep within her psyche.

This is insanity! Missy acknowledged the warning ricocheting around an otherwise emptied skull, but was uninterested. It was stemming from the *WTF are you doing?* sector of her brain. The sage advice went unheeded. She made a mental note to look into the odd cognitive disconnect as soon as possible.

However, possible was entirely impossible at the moment!

The woman standing motionless at this formidable man's behest, breathing gently with eyes cast down, was unrecognizable to Missy. The woman she knew herself to be was independent, fiercely private, and supremely cautious. While it seemed like just yesterday that she'd entered her thirties, she was racing through them at a flat-out gallop. Along the way, she'd managed to raise the most incredible son.

"I can smell you, little one."

The sheer audacity of his words stunned her. Nonetheless, she remained rooted to the spot. The niggling portion of her brain urging caution conceded defeat and crashed to avoid further insult. Every ounce of her attention was focused on him and him alone. Not through downcast eyes, but through her very pores. Everything else was just white noise.

Already, she had no choice...

He spoke conversationally.

"I recognized you the instant I inhaled your scent, my dear. The very essence of your being beckoned to me. You exhibited the most intoxicating combination of desire and distress."

This riveting man wasn't quite done. Smiling benignly into the face of her apoplexy, he continued.

"Most enchanting, however, was the scent of your submission as you turned towards me, your Master."

Submission? Master? She bridled at the unfamiliar terms even as she recognized the forbidden truth of them. She opened her mouth in a weak attempt to object. As if reading her mind, he gently pressed three fingers to her parted, panting lips.

"Do not speak. There will be time for that later. As well, I do not recall giving you permission to do so?"

While there was a teasing note to his words, she was only too aware of the steel enforcing them. Her squirming desisted at once. Her eyes remained compliantly downcast. Missy's head was in the process of exploding with the reality that once again, she was obeying. Without so much as a murmur, she was submitting.

"There's a good girl." She heard his words distinctly, in spite of the ringing in her ears. Missy was positive that the fingers resting against her lips were, in fact, aflame. Their intensity was scalding. Then again, the burn did nothing to distract her from his next directive.

"Now, please open your mouth, my dear."

As if observing from outside of her own body, she was aghast when her lips began to part at the outrageous request. Before she could defend against it, he took full advantage of the invitation. All three digits slid confidently within and made themselves comfortable.

Repeatedly, her gag reflex was triggered. Still, Missy did not move. *Could* not move. She tried to convince herself this was all just an incredibly bizarre daydream. Shortly, she would awaken unscathed to carry on with the predictable monotony of her day and her life.

As soon as he gives me permission, that is!

She felt his fingers pressing impatiently against both lips. Heeding the silent command, she opened wider still. He proceeded to stroke and massage her teeth, cheeks, and tongue, exploring every corner. Her mascara began to run and her eyes to water, and still, she hung on his every syllable.

"You will come to me tonight, little one. Eight o'clock precisely. I suggest that you not be late."

With those words, he removed the three dripping digits from between her lips. Both were mesmerized by the glistening threads of saliva which now stretched between them. He chuckled with delight. She turned crimson with humiliation. After what seemed like forever, he dried his fingers—using her sweater to do so!

Patient as she blinked and swallowed and blinked and

swallowed again, he pressed his business card into her trembling hand. With the tip of a single forefinger, he tilted her chin upwards until their eyes met again.

What she saw changed her world forever...

Chapter 3

Did time actually stand still?

Missy asked herself this question in all seriousness as she collapsed into her car. Her trembling legs were unable to withstand her weight for even a moment longer.

She felt as if she were waking from a long, yet somehow restful, hypnotic trance. *What the hell just happened?* Disoriented, she shook her head, as if doing so might dispel the entire incident. Not to mention the profoundly disconcerting effect it elicited from deep within her.

The card clutched in her hand would not allow for the comfort of self-delusion. There could be no pretending that the incredible sequence of events was simply a phantasmagorical figment of her imagination.

Remnants of the peculiar out of body sensation persisted. Missy lifted the card to her nostrils, closed her eyes, and inhaled deeply. Her tongue explored the interior of her mouth, which had so recently enveloped his fingers, allowing them free reign.

She realized that her senses were subconsciously searching for the tiniest nuance of *him*. Clearly, there was but one logical conclusion. She had completely lost her mind. Things of this nature did not happen. If they did, they certainly didn't happen to *her*. Particularly, not in broad daylight in the parking lot of a grocery store she'd frequented for years.

Friends and neighbors might easily have witnessed the surreal scene of her standing quietly, eagerly suckling on some strange man's hand!

She felt her cheeks burn first with humiliation, and

11

then anger. Missy had been responsible for her own survival from an age when most girls' primary concern was which gown to wear to junior prom!

This was not her first rodeo. Who did this guy think he was? Moreover, who did he think she was?

Submissive...

Missy determined then and there that she had no intention of showing up at the address etched into the card. The same card that was still clenched in her moist palm. She decided to dispose of it without delay.

The very moment she arrived home.

Feeling as though she'd regained some semblance of control, Missy inserted the keys into the ignition and started the engine. It was then that her eyes fell to the clock and a different kind of panic set in.

Chapter 4

Of course, time had not stood still.

In fact, it was so late that Missy began to worry about her son. Why hadn't Christopher texted by now? Sixteen years old with the appetite of two men and a sixteen year old boy, she knew he'd be ravenous.

Looking in several nonsensical nooks and crannies, she eventually located her phone. It was exactly where it belonged, in the side pocket of her over-sized purse. She was shocked to see that not only had her son texted, he'd done so three times. *I must not have heard it over the ringing in my ears.*

With guilt guiding her fingers, she texted him to not worry. She was on her way, dinner in hand. Slipping the car into gear, Missy was home in less than five minutes. Glancing around, she exhaled with relief, hugging her boy a fraction longer and tighter than usual.

Home, sweet home.

As Christopher wriggled free of her clutches, Missy's short-lived relief evaporated. Deep within her soul, she could no longer deny the truth. She may not understand every deviant facet, but the subtle nuances were undeniable. She knew enough to realize that the life she struggled so hard to create was today inexorably altered. A single encounter with a complete stranger had turned it irrevocably upside down.

Her intrinsic desire to please him forced Missy to confront a highly sensitive area of her psyche. An area which previously, was ignored, denied, and snubbed. She'd striven a lifetime, consciously and subconsciously, to blur and obscure it. She believed it was buried deep enough as to be untouchable by anyone. First and foremost, herself.

She was mistaken. The dam had been breached and she hadn't enough fingers to hold back the inevitable deluge. Forbidden secrets were spilling freely into her conscious mind, confirming what she'd always suspected. She didn't belong here. She never really had.

Submissive...

Refusing to allow such disturbing thoughts a foothold in her already distressed mind, Missy got down to the business at hand. She kicked off her heels and went about the soothingly familiar machinations of preparing dinner. Christopher disappeared into his bedroom, facetiously referred to as 'The Cave'.

Deep, dark, and often dank, the cave is filled to overflowing. From conception it seemed, technology was Christopher's 'thing'. He could happily spend days locked away with his computer, to the exclusion of all else. That is, if she allowed it. On a regular basis, Missy would drag her son, kicking and screaming, out of the cave and into the light of day. She would tease him, pointing out fascinating objects which might otherwise have remained foreign.

Objects such as flowers. Trees. Clouds.

It made little impression, however. They both knew it was only a matter of time before Mr. B. Gates would be divvying up office space with her brilliant son.

As she turned to call him to the dinner table, her eyes were drawn to the crumpled, sweat-stained business card. From its lofty place atop the counter, it seemed to mock her. Somehow, it still hadn't made it to the trash bin, in spite of her promise to herself. Missy felt the prickly heat of shame engulf her.

Instantly, she was back in that place where time had stood still. The place where he gazed down upon her lowered head and pressed his card into her sweaty fist. In her mind, his compelling voice informed her again of the time she was expected. She shivered, recalling his 'suggestion' that she not be late.

Yes, she felt the heat of shame. And of indignation. But Missy also felt another kind of heat. There was no mistaking the throbbing heat of desire. She acknowledged for the first time that her pussy was sopping wet. The same went for her panties. And, they weren't *just* wet.

Missy was stunned by the realization that she was blatantly pulsating between her legs. She was swollen, sensitive, and aching with a need the likes of which she'd never experienced. That is, other than in her darkest fantasies.

The portent of this struck her so clearly that it robbed her of what little breath remained in her lungs. Her legs would have given out beneath her if it weren't for the kitchen counter. Thankful for its proximity, she leaned her meager weight against it.

This couldn't be happening. She'd meticulously safeguarded against it. And yet, as much as she may have wished it otherwise, there was no escaping the obvious. His outrageous words vibrated in her mind in perfect harmony with her convulsing pussy.

Submissive...

Suddenly, Christopher burst from the cave and straight into the kitchen, growling and salivating like the starving bear he resembled. Dragging her attention back to the present, she shook off her dazed reverie.

Not quick enough. He stopped dead in his bear tracks

when he saw the stricken look on her face.

"What's wrong, mom?"

Missy smiled reassuringly at her beautiful son.

"Nothing at all baby. Other than I forgot to mention that I have a date tonight. I'm sorry hon, but you'll have to eat without me."

With that, she set out a plate of cheeseburgers and a pitcher of lemonade, his favorite meal. He no longer bothered to debate the accompanying broccoli. Resigned, he munched the detested greenery.

Mouth full, Christopher peppered his mother with questions about this rare and impending date. Lacking acceptable answers, Missy sidestepped the inquisition as best she could with benign generalities. Glancing once more at the clock, she kissed the top of his head and dashed from the kitchen. The last thing she saw was the smile that lit up her son's face like a Christmas tree.

Chapter 5

While Missy may have preferred her breasts a cup size or two larger, the truth was they fit her body perfectly. What stood out, quite literally, were her thick, infuriatingly sensitive nipples. Catching a glimpse of her profile in the full-length mirror, Missy turned to view herself with newly-opened eyes.

The image gazing intently back at her was a petite five foot three with a lean, athletic build. She was still dressed head to toe in black. Black and unadorned was the prescribed dress code at Boutique Ebony&Ivory, the upscale shop where she worked.

Even so, her nipples were sharply delineated, poking through both her bra and loose fitting shirt. Secretly, Missy wondered if other women's nipples were as hyper-sensitive as her own. She hoped not, for their sakes.

It would require a complete lack of self awareness on her part to not grasp that men were attracted to her. From the time she was a flat chested tomboy, the primary adjective used to describe her was 'sexy'. While she didn't necessarily understand it, her concern was not the men's excessive interest in her. Her concern lay with her utter lack of interest in any of them.

Probing her translucent hazel eyes in the mirror, she confessed to herself that she always knew the true genesis of her apathy towards men. Until today, however, she thought that truth was successfully compartmentalized and suppressed.

She was wrong.

Missy could barely recall the last time she accepted a date. Not that the surreal events of this afternoon could be construed in any way, shape, or form as being asked out on a date. Her acceptance was never any part of the equation. She had been summoned, pure and simple. There appeared to be no question as to her arrival. Somehow, it was a given.

Submissive...

"Date, my ass!" Missy spat the words. At the same time, she climbed out of her work clothes and peeled off her sodden panties. Standing nude in the doorway of her closet, she assessed her wardrobe choices. She wasn't surprised that precious few seemed appropriate for such an 'occasion'.

Between her lack of attire and the hunger her body was shamelessly emitting, she didn't pause to wonder what she was getting herself into. In truth, there was no need. Deep down, she already knew the answer to that treacherous question. She knew the instant she felt the magnetic pull of that enigmatic man. A man she was clearly incapable of defending against. His eyes had imprisoned her, irrevocably binding her to him and testifying both to her nature and to her future.

The term 'soul-mate' sprang to mind, but didn't quite fit. Soul-*Master* seemed a far more accurate description. She wasn't capable of processing this data at the time due to the sudden malfunctioning of her good and common sense. However, there'd been plenty of time to process it since.

Still, here she stood, wondering what she might wear to please him.

Please him? She refused to dwell on the treacherous words which sprang so readily to mind. Instead, she distracted herself by donning a cute floral skirt that came to rest modestly a few inches above her knees. She added a matching midnight blue tank and the sexiest heels she owned. She very much yearned to take a long, hot bath, but knew it was impossible under the stringent time constraints. Missy completed the ensemble with fresh, dry panties.

It would have to do.

After brushing her thick auburn hair, freshening her make-up, and adding a hint of cologne, she wavered. But, only for a moment. With a deep breath, she scooped up the rumpled business card, a little annoyed that it hadn't found its way into the garbage on its own.

Although it wasn't possible, the card seemed to pulsate in her palm. She'd have sworn to it. Missy stopped short, armed with the surety that before today she'd enjoyed a fairly firm grip on reality.

If earlier she wasn't able to grasp that she was standing at a critical crossroads, she was now fully cognizant of the fact. She was also keenly aware that, already, it was too late to turn back.

Something was changed, and irrevocably so. For the first time that she could recall, Missy felt swathed in a blanket of sweet serenity. Incrementally, it was taking the place of her chronic and often overwhelming anxiety. The same anxiety that medication failed to dull.

Master...

The combination on the vault containing her deepest, darkest secrets had tumbled into place. Now, those secrets were strewn hither and yon, exposed to the glaring light of truth and consciousness. There was nothing left to hide. She was found out.

At long last, she understood that she wasn't bad or wrong. Nor was she defective. She was *submissive*. She rolled the word around in her mind and on her tongue, tasting of its legitimacy as she might the rarest of delicacies.

Smiling softly, Missy kissed her son goodbye. Gently, she closed the door to her home, and to her past, behind her.

Chapter 6

James Colton paced his office like a caged animal. Lines of anguish were etched into his forehead and pangs of guilt gnawed at his gut. Missy weighed heavily on his mind. His torment had nothing to do with any concern of her not arriving. Just the opposite, in fact.

He berated himself for not leaving her alone. For not allowing her to walk away without learning of his existence. Most of all, he didn't feel it was his right to expose her true nature, even to her. Or perhaps, especially to her.

It was obvious that she struggled to deny it. A struggle that was apparent to him in every nuance of her being. A struggle lost forever the instant she looked into his eyes.

She'd had no choice...

And he knew it. James recognized her like a lion recognizes the gazelle that is to be cut from the herd. James stopped his pointless pacing in front of the fireplace. Bending, he began to go through the motions of building a fire. Without skipping a beat, his mind continued to replay the cataclysmic events that his own words and actions set into motion.

He admitted, he'd been selfish. He wanted what he once had, fully aware that it was nigh on impossible. He believed there was a higher probability of getting struck twice by lightning. He yearned for more than any man had a right to ask for.

And yet, only a few short hours ago and against all odds, lightning *did* strike for the second time. The petite, harried girl in the check-out line jump started his heart and his imagination. She was breathtaking as she scrambled to collect her change, her groceries, and her wits.

Submissive...

And he knew it. A scowl crossed his face when it suddenly occurred to him that he hadn't lit a fire since Angeline, his angel, died. Not once since burying the woman he loved more than he'd imagined possible. *Was it really almost three years since that unfathomable day?* How could it be that every yesterday felt like a lifetime, yet three years felt like only yesterday?

He would never forget the condemning eyes of Angeline's inconsolable parents. They glared at him from the opposite side of her freshly dug grave. They needed a scapegoat to assuage their unbearable grief, and James was only too congenial in providing them one. After all, they could never blame him as much as he blamed himself. Angeline belonged to him and with him. It was incomprehensible that he wasn't able to protect her.

It didn't matter that she died from a sudden, freak asthma attack. Nor did it make any impact when the doctors assured him there was nothing anyone could have done. He was not anyone. He was her *Master.* It was his responsibility to keep her safe from harm. He'd failed.

If Angeline's parents needed someone to blame, James wasn't about to deflect their anger. In fact, he was so besotted with grief that he welcomed it.

Tom and Maxine were never able to understand their baby's contentment with what they considered her 'lowly station' in life. They fretted over her apparent pride in a dark and mysterious alternative lifestyle. They were unable to see past the ever-present choker, or collar, that was padlocked around her dainty neck.

Just as it was on the day she was buried.

The bruises on her once pristine knees were another bone of contention. They could not understand why Angeline didn't cover them, at least. They were appalled when she made no effort whatsoever to disguise them. Still, Tom and Maxine refused to accept the truth. From their perspective, it could only be *his* doing. It *had* to be his Svengali-like influence. Their baby girl would *never* put up with such obviously demeaning treatment!

Although Angeline assured them again and again that her 'station' in life afforded her great happiness, they remained unconvinced. They considered James nothing more than a twisted deviant. A deviant that somehow managed to brainwash their sweet and innocent daughter. What other explanation could there be for her seemingly blind obedience? She literally worshipped the ground he walked on.

James snapped out of his reverie and stood to stretch cramped legs. He glanced at the clock on his desk. It wouldn't be long now.

Deciding a drink was in order, he crossed to the sidebar and poured himself a generous cognac. Performing the task by rote, his attention was drawn back to earlier that evening. In his mind's eye, he relived every incredulous, debaucherous detail. The rich, caramel colored liquid of the finest Remy Martin XO was left to swirl unappreciated in its snifter.

Missy would never suspect that their fateful encounter was as momentous for him as it was for her. She exuded a pure and natural submissiveness that was like nectar to a bee. James had never encountered such in forty-seven years on this earth.

Another man might have perceived nothing out of the

ordinary. Other than her obvious physical beauty, of course. But to James, there was no mistaking what lay dormant beneath. Her attempts at concealment were both adorable and utterly transparent. Every step she took screamed out to him. Every tilt of her head begged for his consideration. Every shrug of her shoulders implored him to reach out and take what he intuitively knew was meant to be his.

James took a long pull at his drink. He was forced to admit that even Angeline didn't elicit such sharp pangs of instant recognition and desire. Certainly not on such a subliminal level.

Contemplating the veracity of subjecting a second innocent girl to his Dominant ways was now a moot question. It was no longer worthy of either his time or his energy. The deed was done. The only direction available was forward.

In truth, James relished the journey. He could almost see Missy kneeling motionless at his feet. Her back would be arched and her shoulders pressed back, impelling the chest respectfully forward. He could almost taste of her desire for his attention and approval as it emanated from her every pore.

His desire would be for those full, velvety lips to remain exposed for his viewing pleasure. Or, for any other pleasure that he saw fit.

His cock hardened far too quickly at the delectable images. It came as quite a surprise after years of self-imposed celibacy. To him, the act of sex was simply a natural by product of a properly orchestrated Dominant/submissive relationship. It was never the primary focus. For James and men of his mindset, the key lay in the mental and spiritual connection.

In their domain, this is known as 'power exchange'.

The ultimate goal? To establish a mutual trust so profound that inter-dependency was something to be desired, not feared and condemned. A trust so multifaceted that if the act of physical sex were, for whatever reason, no longer available, the mind/spirit dynamic would remain vibrant and intact.

A soft tapping at the front door heralded Missy's arrival and caused his eyes to turn to the hands of the clock once again. The minute indicator was just turning over to thirteen. Thirteen minutes past the hour. He was sure he told her to not be late.

His displeasure was evidenced only by an almost imperceptible tightening of his brow, and a slight upturn at one corner of his mouth. An observer might assume it to be the beginning of a smile. The observer would be wrong.

Thirteen was *not* going to be her lucky number.

Chapter 7

She was late. *Again.*

The only sound besides the ringing in Missy's ears was that of her breathing, which was coming fast and hard. Chest heaving, she observed her hands begin to tremble as they gripped the steering wheel. She was known to suffer from panic attacks in the past. This was not a panic attack.

She squinted beyond the windshield and through the darkness at his large, imposing home. She'd done so well, too! Having gathered what remained of her wits about her, she was somehow able to focus on the GPS instructions. Missy navigated the unfamiliar streets of the upscale neighborhood without incident.

That is, until a sudden and blinding flash of clarity struck, forcing her to pull the little Nissan to the curb. That had been her final opportunity to turn back. She realized then that if she continued down the path she was on, there would be fewer and fewer egress opportunities.

She was in unfamiliar territory, traversing untested terrain. She didn't need a GPS to tell her that.

Then why was it that she felt her only course of action was to go directly to him? What was compelling her to throw caution to the wind and hurtle headlong into the dark and undiscovered? She was speeding towards a mysterious man of whom she knew nothing, yet identified with on a level she'd hoped to never explore.

Deep down, Missy knew the reason: Luke Terrence Weaver, her ex-husband and Christopher's father. Well, sperm donor, at least.

She'd done everything in her power to walk the straight

and narrow path that society kept impeccably groomed. She was the proverbial good girl, marriage and babies and happily ever after. The stuff of fairy tales. And, doesn't every little girl adore a good fairy tale?

She'd poured every ounce of herself into a life that never quite fit, wanting desperately to don the 'one-size-fits-all' existence and have it suit her to a T. Instead, it was more like wearing a pair of pantyhose two sizes too small. Forever.

Not impossible. Not even life-threatening. Just unrelentingly irritating and confining. Missy determined that she could, and would, endure the suffocating discomfort. There were worse things in life. She counted being different amongst them.

Yes, she was more than willing to bend. But, Luke did his damnedest to break her. Over time, he'd almost succeeded. The high school football hero that made the young girls swoon didn't even attempt to fulfill his potential.

Once upon a time, he was capable of much more than just scoring touchdowns. Luke was reputed to be a miracle worker when it came to fixing almost any make or model of vehicle. He had big plans to become a master mechanic and spoke of franchising cutting edge repair shops from sea to shining sea.

Nobody doubted that he possessed the skills to make it happen. What he didn't possess, however, was a single iota of commitment or self-accountability. Luke wanted immediate gratification and he wanted it *now!* The dream turned into just another nightmare, washed away in a shining sea of 'whine' and vodka. The same sea that claimed his looks and once impressive physique.

Yes, he could have grown into the kind of man that

women dreamed about. Instead, he chose to simply grow into an older, meaner, and pathetically unemployable version of his former self.

Truth be told, Missy was more than a little afraid of him, although she would never admit it in front of their son. When they were married, Luke was a five-foot-nine, hundred-and-ninety pound drunken bully. In the years since the divorce, he devolved into an intimidating two-hundred-and-forty pound drunken stalker.

Too often, Luke came around for money to buy booze. Ten dollars here, twenty dollars there. Grabbing her here, shoving her there. She learned the hard way that it was easiest to just give it to him.

Twice, she'd called the police. Twice, they'd politely took her report, and filed it, doing nothing.

"Terribly sorry ma'am, but until you or your son are threatened directly, or your property is damaged, our hands are tied. Of course, this report will be filed along with the first. At least then they're both on record, just in case something more serious occurs."

"Here's our contact information and some pamphlets. Don't hesitate to call if there's anything else we can do. Have a nice day, ma'am."

Missy had accepted the pamphlets. She'd never called again.

Chapter 8

She'd felt much more composed then, as she sat ruminating on the side of a dark, unfamiliar street. Inexplicably, she was infused with the same sensation of tranquility that calmed her earlier in James' presence. The same feeling had enveloped her just as her lips parted to flagrantly taste of his fingers. She remembered how they caressed the deepest recesses of her mouth. And her mind.

Recollecting these powerful sensations, any remaining doubt evaporated. She was left with only one other eye-opening realization. The fresh panties that she so recently slipped on were nothing short of drenched. Prying one hand from the steering wheel, she reached between her legs. She was appalled to find the lips of her swollen pussy pressing wantonly against the thin, straining fabric!

Not to mention that her distended nipples were chafing maddeningly against the material of her brassiere. Missy could not deny the evidence one second longer. Her body was saying what her mind had refused to contemplate for the majority of her life.

Submissive...

Deciding it was high time to pay attention, she resolutely shifted the car into drive and pointed it in the direction of James' house.

Where she now sat frozen, staring blindly at the imposing fortress, fortitude wilting. Gulping air in a final effort to muster her nerve, she exited the safety of her vehicle to ascend the rounded steps to her destiny. Missy barely managed to uncurl her fingers from the knocker before the wooden door flew open.

His hand was a blur as it shot out, securing itself firmly around her throat...

Chapter 9

"You're late, my dear."

The slow, sardonic drawl was completely incongruous with his actions. Even if his hand were not exerting a steady pressure at her throat, Missy would have been rendered speechless at the sight of him.

The interior lights shone softly behind him, infusing him with an almost dreamlike aura. He filled the doorway, accentuating the considerable difference in their sizes. *Why didn't I notice how muscular he is?* Even casually dressed in jeans and untucked tee, he would turn heads anywhere.

Missy, however, was in no position for head turning. His hand was scalding against the flesh of her throat. As if in response, her pulse throbbed against the flesh of his hand. Without another word she was impelled forward, out of the darkness and into the light. It was as though he was pulling her free of her self-imposed prison.

As James bolted the massive door behind them, a curious mantra played over and over in Missy's mind.

I'm home...

She was disallowed further opportunity to explore this unnerving concept. There were far more pressing circumstances to consider. With his hand still firmly at her throat, James insinuated one thigh between the two of hers. In one effortless motion, he pressed her back against the now sealed doorway. Removing his thigh, their physical contact was again limited to a single powerful hand encircling her tiny, pulsating throat.

At arm's length, James assessed her silently, unhurriedly, and thoroughly. If she was incapable of absorbing much in the way of detail, James inundated his senses with her. She was truly an intoxicating rose. He noted that she held her eyes cast downwards as if instinctual, and was delighted. Not only was she beautiful and bright, she was even more submissive than he imagined. If that were possible.

Missy began to fidget under the close scrutiny, forcing his hand to tighten its grip ever-so-slightly. It took but a moment for comprehension to dawn. Her squirming came to an immediate halt, allowing him to continue his close inspection.

He observed the flush of her cheek and the heave of her chest. He noticed her nipples, hard and straining through both bra and shirt. He knew with absolute certainty that she was wet.

James reached out slowly with his free hand, capturing one thick nipple between his fingers and squeezing just until she whimpered. He did not let go nor did he loosen his grip. She remained motionless, moaning intermittently. He was sure she was remembering his wordless admonition of just a few moments ago.

"You disrespect me with your tardiness, little one. It would never occur to me to disrespect you in such a manner. You will learn this evening that disobedience cannot and will not be tolerated."

With those words, he literally felt her breath catch in her throat. He could almost see her mind as it began to cartwheel from her control. He knew that, this time, it had nothing to do with the pressure at her throat. He stood above her with one hand encircling that lovely column, the other firmly affixed to her now pounding nipple.

And yet, *he* was scolding *her* for being disrespectful!

James was certain that in any other time and with any other man, she would not hesitate to shut him down. Security would have been called long before this pleasant juncture, without doubt. He could almost hear her laughing with disdain at such unmitigated arrogance as she marched out the door, slamming it behind her with a flourish.

Instead of that drama, here she stood, motionless before him. Accepting his truth as her own. He could feel her pulse slow against the palm of his hand. Her breathing steadied as she gradually arrived at the same realization. He released his grip from her throat and observed closely.

Her head tilted back. Unwittingly, she exposed the tender flesh of her just released throat for his viewing pleasure. A soft moan escaped her lips. A wolfish grin appeared on his.

Whether her conscious mind was fully aware of it or not, her body was blatantly offering itself to him. While he smiled at this most telling of displays, he certainly wasn't surprised.

Submissive...

James was well versed in the trials and tribulations of the submissive woman. When she unexpectedly finds herself exactly where she is meant to be, the relief and release can be so intense as to be almost unbearable.

He empathized with her years of self-imposed isolation and denial. He felt her anxiety as she slowly arrived at the realization that she was different from the other girls. Fundamentally different.

It pained him to imagine her shame at this wretchedly unfair life sentence. How terrifying it must be to inhabit a world that doesn't understand and refuses to accept.

'Different' has never been well tolerated societally. Once upon a time women who were considered different would be burned at the stake. Or stoned in the streets.

Chapter 10

When James abruptly removed his hand from her throat, Missy's reaction was quite different from what she would have expected of herself only yesterday. Instead of outrage and indignation, she was mortified to find herself moaning in anguish at the sudden loss of contact.

Before she knew it, she was arching her throat towards him in silent surrender. Her nostrils flared, seeking out his already recognizable scent. James emanated an irresistible combination of fine cognac, faint cologne, and powerful male pheromones. Missy would swear to its distinct familiarity.

Master...

Her inflamed nipple remained ensconced between his persistent fingers. The all consuming combination of pain and pleasure shot through her body in two opposite directions. Both left her equally faint with need and laser focused on him.

One unrelenting current ran from her tender nipple directly to her brain, the voltage sufficient to induce the most exquisite aura of submissiveness. The other ran unswervingly to her already engorged pussy, voltage diminished not a single iota. Missy's head all but exploded from the surplus of stimuli.

Upon hearing his hushed directive to open her mouth, intense memories of that afternoon penetrated her dazed mind. Immediately and without trepidation, Missy moved to do his bidding.

How could it be that she, a self-possessed and dignified woman, found herself in such mind boggling circumstances? Worse, how was it possible that the same self-possessed and dignified woman was actually looking forward to this man's next wickedly scandalous directive? Looking forward with what could only be described as throbbing excitement, no less.

Missy wondered how much longer it would be until her legs simply gave out from under her. *When, not if.*

That would be her last rational thought. All sensical supposition was henceforth disabled. The fingers clamped around her pounding nipple relinquished their stranglehold to some small degree. They now alternated between gentle tweaks and brusque twists.

Missy could actually envision the pulsating bolts of white light that were being masterfully transmitted to the core of her being. She was convinced that James could see them just as clearly. After all, he caused them.

The fingers of his free hand were at her parted lips, opening them further. James reached within the cavern of her hot, wet mouth and without hesitation, secured a firm hold on her tongue. She felt herself recoil in shock, the movement causing sharp discomfort. Even so, he did not relinquish his grip. In fact, the more she attempted to pull away, the tighter it became.

Missy's eyes began to tear. Once again, he'd wordlessly conveyed his wishes, and once again, Missy capitulated. Motionless and compliant now, she listened to the peculiar ringing in her ears as he drew her tongue from the safe confines of her mouth. He stretched it until it could go no further.

She would wonder later if he were actually humming, or whether it was just her inflamed imagination. In any case, it was at this awkward juncture that James *allowed* her to look directly into his eyes. Her entire body ignited with scalding hot shame as her eyes slowly rose to meet his.

She was utterly helpless to prevent the saliva that was dripping onto his fingers from her hyper extended tongue. If possible, his eyes were even more riveting than the first time she found herself held captive within them. The loving acceptance that emanated from them suffused her. Missy's heart melted.

Without breaking eye contact, he leaned forward and crudely spat upon her distended tongue, co-mingling his saliva with hers. Considering that she was long past disbelief and well into the liberating glow of acquiescence, she barely flinched.

The kiss that followed was so unexpectedly sweet as to bring another kind of tears to her eyes: tears of joy. James kissed her like she'd never been kissed, touching not only her lips, but her soul. Entangling not only their tongues, but their destinies.

He kissed her until she was panting into his mouth, unwittingly attempting to grind her inflamed pussy against his leg. James easily held her at bay simply by applying or relieving pressure to her nipple. All she knew for sure at that exquisite moment was that she wanted more.

No, she *needed* more.

For the third time in a single twenty-four hour period, she was floating in the warmest, rarest aura of absolute peace. She was soon to learn that this all encompassing glow of well being was called *sub-space*.

Sub-space was a state of being that Missy would come to beg for. Literally. She felt it the moment James shut the door on the outside world and introduced her to her destiny. It was uncomplicated.

Master...

Chapter 11

Missy wasn't the only participant transformed by the events of the evening. Not even James, an experienced, worldly Dominant, could have predicted the outcome. The simple act of bending to kiss this bewitching creature's opened mouth elicited a response within him which was nothing short of staggering.

Tasting of her unleashed longing and unrestrained submission triggered a fierce desire within James to protect this woman. He would keep her safe from the judgment of a sexually repressed culture that would frown upon such an exceptional creature.

Missy was that rare treasure whose nature was to serve and whose pleasure lay in structure and approval. What had been missing from her life was a man she could trust, a Master she could worship. One who would adore and appreciate her in return.

Was it just that afternoon that he was drawn to her on an instinctual level so profound that the impact prompted him to pursue her to her car? His mission was to confront her with her own submissive nature. He neglected to factor in the basic principle that for every action, there is an equal and opposite reaction. What he failed to predict was that she would pour every particle of her 'self' into every nuance of his consciousness.

His spittle was shared between them like the sweetest of nectar, binding them incontrovertibly together. A twinge of guilt gripped him as his tongue reached for, and ravished Missy's. Willfully, he endeavored to summon Angeline's beautiful face to his mind's eye. He was unable.

After three long years of mourning, had his lingering self-reproach been eradicated? After three long years, was he finally free to love another?

Breaking off the kiss, James released her nipple and took a few moments to regain control of his emotions. Not to mention his raging erection. If he felt any turmoil within, his calm exterior belied its existence. He observed as she fell back against the door, mouth agape—this time of its own volition. Her breathing was shallow and audible. Her need was palpable to every one of his five senses.

Both nipples were clearly delineated through the thin top. The left one, however, was pleasantly engorged due to the extra attention it was paid. He could virtually see it pulsing in time to her heartbeat as blood rushed to the deprived tip.

James felt his need to dominate this waif of a girl intensify at the same pace as his feelings towards her deepened. He anticipated with delight the journey that lay ahead.

The profound and absolute trust shared between a Master and his submissive is difficult if not impossible to define. It can defy words and challenge time. It can transcend the physical. While it was of his nature to discover, explore, and ultimately push limits, he was also acutely aware that trust and timing were paramount.

Baby steps, James, baby steps...

Smiling, he reached out to stroke Missy's disheveled hair and damp cheek. She gazed up at him, adoration glowing from her eyes.

"You've comported yourself well, little one. But, I can't have you thinking that good behavior somehow cancels out the bad, now can I?"

He very much enjoyed watching her eyes grow to the size of saucers. Still, she uttered not a word, forcing him to repeat himself.

"Now, can I?"

"I...I guess not."

James was delighted. Those three little words spoke volumes. He allowed her lack of formality to slide. For the moment.

"You've earned yourself a good spanking for your lack of punctuality, wouldn't you agree, my dear?"

When no answer was forthcoming yet again, he repeated the words slowly and patiently. He might have been addressing a beloved child just a little slow on the uptake.

"Well, my pretty? Would you or would you not agree?"

"I would agree...I guess."

Again James was pleased when she squeaked out the almost inaudible response. This time, however, he wanted more.

"You shall call me sir from now on, as is your place, whore! Perhaps one day you shall earn the right to call me Master. We shall have to see about that, won't we?"

When Missy nodded dumbly in response, the displeasure on his face must have been enough to spur her into finding her voice.

"Yes, sir!"

James smiled. Her desire to please him overrode her shock at his words.

"There's my good girl!"

There was no mistaking the joy that flashed in her eyes in response to the verbal reward. What came next however, was quick to turn that joy into alarmed apprehension.

"I'm thinking that because you were thirteen minutes late, you should have thirteen strokes on each delectable buttock. That is, unless you feel that you require more in order to understand the importance of punctuality?"

This time, there was no mistaking her stunned intake of breath. His ominous words appeared to have the same impact as a jab to her solar plexus. Disbelief was plain on her face. James could read her jumbled thoughts simply by observing the emotions playing out across her beautiful, distorted features.

"No, sir. Thirteen strokes will be fine, thank you, sir."

His cock hardened to still greater dimensions as Missy not only condoned her own punishment, but thanked him for it. Pre-cum oozed thickly from the swollen head.

James smiled again.

Chapter 12

No sir. Thirteen strokes will be fine, thank you, sir.

Missy felt her own clumsy lips form every syllable. She heard every unfathomable word as it was spoken. Still, she was having difficulty accepting that it was she that was speaking them.

What had happened to the distrustful recluse who found it necessary to safeguard herself against the world? How had it come to be that she was speaking with humble deference to, what amounted to, a complete stranger? A stranger who pinned her to the door by the throat, bruised her tender nipple, and kissed her like never before in her life. A stranger who politely inquired how many 'strokes' she felt she 'deserved'.

How could she rationalize to herself, or anyone else, the warm glow of belonging that enveloped her when he even glanced in her direction? How could she explain the unprecedented absence of inner conflict and anxiety? This man was the furthest thing from a stranger even if they had only just 'met'.

Missy had imitated the salmon her entire life. She'd swum upstream, against the natural current. Instinctively, she'd sought a suitable mate that she almost hoped didn't exist. Willing to die trying or go without, she'd gone without —fully expecting to die trying.

Until today.

James spoke, his voice mandating her absolute attention. The deep resonance soothed her senses, refocusing her awareness to where it seemed most content. *On him!*

Curling a lock of her hair around his finger, he

instructed her to find her way to his kitchen. She was to return with an appropriate instrument with which he might inflict her punishment. He must have noticed her facial features as they transformed from slack acquiescence to appalled disbelief. Missy was mortified at the thought of aiding and abetting in her own chastisement!

She couldn't fathom why her traitorous sex gushed at the idea. Unperturbed, James continued, his tone ominous.

"Do not disappoint me, my dear. Rest assured, should you return with a feather duster, it shall only afford me an excellent excuse to escalate your punishment. Not that the prospect of such is in any way distasteful. Quite the contrary."

Taking her by both arms, he turned her in the direction of the kitchen. Before releasing her, he cinched her drooping shoulders firmly back, impressing upon her the proper carriage he expected from his submissive. Shoulders back, chin up, breasts pressed exaggeratedly forward.

Got it.

Satisfied, he patted her bottom familiarly, impelling her onward. She felt his eyes follow her as she took the first tentative steps towards his kitchen, and her fate.

As she teetered unsteadily along the unfamiliar hallway, there was no denying the shocking truth that was coursing through her hyper sensitized mind and body.

She could hardly wait...

Chapter 13

Awaiting her return, James refilled his tumbler before sliding open a closet door. He searched past the boxes of obsolete paperwork and old tax documents that all but obscured the one item he sought. Delighted to locate the ancient, long-forgotten ironing board, he freed it from years of confinement.

He vaguely heard Missy. She was rummaging through kitchen cupboards and drawers in her search for the perfect utensil. The utensil which, in short order, would be the instrument of her castigation.

Again he felt his long denied cock stir in his jeans, head damp and sticky from pre-cum. It had been leaking since well before she arrived. His raging hard-on was all the more cumbersome as he bent down to rest the narrow end of the ironing board against the sofa cushions. Leaving the wider end on the floor, he created an almost perfect forty-five degree angle. Task complete, he rose just as Missy reentered the room.

Again he was struck by her beauty. He marveled at the innate submissiveness which she unknowingly displayed with her every step.

It always amazed him to hear tales from submissive women who swore that no one *ever* suspected their true nature. At least, not until that fateful day on which they happened to meet their Dominant equivalent. The Yang to their yin, Top to their bottom, Lead to their follow. The one man who saw past their defenses and straight to the heart of the matter.

Straight to the heart of the true submissive!

To the undiscerning eye, it is the Dominant who has absolute control. To the uninformed, the 'poor' naive submissive seems nothing more than a mistreated prisoner. Very much like Angeline's parents, who found it easier to believe that misguided notion than the truth.

The truth was that wild horses could not have dragged their daughter from his side!

While there are toxic relationships in every lifestyle, it is generally accepted that submissive women are of above average intelligence and accomplishment. They are by no means the lesser partner in the relationship, but a full and contributing half. In their own submissive way and from their proper submissive place, of course.

A Dominant without his submissive is as bereft as a submissive without her Master. The critical distinction was that the Dom fared better in a society where dominance was a sought after attribute. In fact, it was right up there with assertiveness and leadership.

Submissiveness, on the other hand, was not a sought after trait; not by society nor by corporate America. It was mistakenly likened to passivity and meekness, a common misconception.

Undoubtedly, James' natural personality traits impacted his career in a positive manner. He was rapidly propelled from sales floor to corner executive office in just under fourteen years; an unprecedented feat in the dog-eat-dog world of sales and marketing. His meteoric rise was attested to by numerous plaques, awards, vacations, and, last but not least—bonuses. Bonuses substantial enough to leave him financially stress free.

Easily, he was able to indulge his passing whims, as well

as Angeline's. He took small comfort in knowing that she wanted for nothing right up until the day she died.

Turning his attention back to the present, he drank in the vision before him. Disheveled and delectable were only two delicious words that sprang to mind. He crooked his index finger at Missy, leaving no room for misinterpretation. She moved compliantly forward, halting before him.

Seeking approval, she offered forth a slotted spatula. Holding it away from herself between two fingers, it might have been a poisonous insect about to bite her.

And bite her it would. James smiled at the analogy and at Missy as he removed the tool from her quivering hand. He then made quite the production of testing its veracity. She watched entranced, somewhere between shock and resigned disbelief, as he whipped it through the air.

"This will work splendidly. Well done little one!"

Again, her eyes lit up at his words of praise. Had she feathers, she'd be preening. However, the proud light in her eyes flickered when he directed her to straddle the ironing board. He knew she was still processing the bizarre instruction when he raised his voice, becoming decidedly less ambiguous.

"Get that sweet ass spread wide across that ironing board, and do not make me repeat myself a third time!"

She all but scampered over to where the ironing board awaited, clearly perplexed as to what was expected of her. She looked imploringly over her shoulder at him, uncertainty shimmering in her luminous eyes.

Always the gentleman, he set his glass on the desk, took her hand, and assisted her to her knees. Before she could pull away in protest, he reached beneath her shirt and expertly unclasped her bra. Politely, James requested that she remove it.

"I never want you to insult me by wearing one of those in my presence again."

Swinging the offending article of underclothing contemptuously from one finger, he reached down to maul her now loosed tits. They bounced and quivered unrestrained just beneath the thin top, nipples hard as bullets. He didn't even try to mask the satisfaction on his face.

"Look up at me, little one, I did not ask you to lower your eyes."

There was no denying the pleasure he received from witnessing the burning indignity clouding her hazel pools as she raised them to meet his. Blood surge in his veins. *What is it about a woman on her knees obeying my every desire?* Whatever it was, it stirred his heart and roused his cock. He paused in order to bask in the long overdue pleasure of the moment. The sights and sounds were equally mouth watering.

Finally, James helped her to lay belly down on the board. Missy's head was on an incline towards the sofa, her arms and legs wrapped tightly around the benign household item. Concerned for her every comfort, James was careful to arrange her tits so they hung freely off each side.

James perused his handiwork, deciding it would make the perfect first image for a *very* special photo album. He was a big photo buff. Reluctantly, he decided to set aside that tempting indulgence for another day; the day she willingly returned to him. In the meantime, there was plenty to keep him occupied.

Humming softly, he bent down to lift her skirt,

exposing the rounded cheeks of her bottom. The little panties had long ago given up trying to contain the liquid evidence of her need. There was naught to be done as it leaked profusely, oozing down her thighs.

"You are a nasty little whore, aren't you? Just look at this sloppy cunt!"

Considering that the ironing board greatly inhibited her ability to draw breath, the gasp of shock which emitted from her was truly impressive.

He used one hand and very little effort to tear the sopping panties from her body. The other hand was pressed firmly and deliberately between her shoulder blades. She began to wriggle self-consciously under his flagrant scrutiny, as he knew she would.

When all was again calm, other than the sound of her ragged breath, James picked up the spatula and began to hum...

Chapter 14

By that point, her cerebral acuity wasn't worth the gray matter it was imprinted upon. Missy clung half naked and humiliated to the ironing board, awaiting the punishment she'd agreed she deserved. One thing was crystal clear: she *was* a nasty little whore and deep down had *always* been a nasty little whore. Exactly as James said!

Growing up, she would listen as the other girls spoke in hushed tones of their most intimate fantasies. Making sweet love to a handsome lover on the banks of the Seine or being swept breathlessly off their feet by the sexiest movie star in La-La-Land were common themes.

Hers, in comparison, were anything *but* common. Her nasty fantasies consisted of being bound and gagged and ravished and used. They entailed discipline and rituals and rules and obedience. She hated to admit it, even to herself, but—anal sex was the 'norm', not the exception.

Above all, however, her fantasies were suffused with love. In them, she felt cherished, protected and adored. Now, how could that be wrong?

Submissive...

'Whore' seemed a compliment of the highest order in his world. When James used the socially abhorrent term, it warmed her heart as much as any endearment. More so, perhaps. Only where he was concerned, the single-syllabic 'description' fit her like a Giorgio Armani glove.

The evidence was clear. Here she lay in a panic, awaiting the dreaded first blow. Yet her juices continued to leak from a shamefully engorged pussy and down already slick thighs.

Whore!

The thought of his eyes penetrating that most intimate of places, bearing witness to the accuracy of his words, scorched her face with utter mortification. In addition, it caused her pussy to ooze all the more.

Whore!

She was deep within herself, giving herself over to the emotional and physical stimuli. She no longer resisted or questioned. When the first blow was finally administered, she screamed and almost tumbled to the floor. She was positive that the tender, virgin flesh of her left butt cheek was on fire. The muscles quivered and contracted in urgent response to the insult.

One arm also flew from the ironing board, hand pressed against the floor in a perilous struggle for balance. She would never be able to endure twelve more strokes on that already throbbing cheek and then thirteen on the other. *Never!*

Yet, instead of putting an end to the preposterous state of affairs, Missy yanked the offending appendage from the floor and once again embraced the board as mandated. Instead of leaping from the board and racing for the door, she hoped instead that James hadn't noticed the momentary gaffe.

But, of course, he had. The humming came to an abrupt halt. She watched as his booted feet passed within her line of vision. They made a sharp about-face before he sank into the sofa with a long, heavy sigh. One boot began to tap. His disappointment was obvious.

All regard for the throbbing pain he'd just inflicted upon her person was forgotten. Missy was forced to acknowledge that her only concern at that moment was for *his* happiness. More to the point, she desired that he be happy with *her*, his 'whore'!

James used the spatula to lift her chin from the ironing board, enabling her to see the suspected disappointment reflected in his eyes. Missy was devastated.

"I expected more from you, little one."

His words were so soft, she strained to hear.

"It is not my wish to punish you. It is simply my duty as your caring Master. Anything less would leave me derelict in my duties and you a confused little slut with no idea of what's expected. We wouldn't want that, now would we?"

Without waiting for his flagrant words to register with her sluggish brain, he went on.

"Now, my dear, I think it only appropriate that you present me your loveliest smile and thank me for being ever-so-attentive to your needs."

Thank him? Smile pretty? Surely he was joking? As the seconds ticked inexorably by, she realized that he was not. Missy struggled to meet his expectant gaze as she arranged her swollen lips into a distorted facsimile of a smile.

"Yes, sir. Th...thank you sir."

Her words came out as a high-pitched squeak.

He clapped his hands together, obviously delighted with her ability to catch on.

"Good girl! Now, raise that pretty ass as high as it will go for me. That's it."

James pushed further still.

"Higher, please. I want to see it waving in the air, begging for the punishment it so richly deserves. And, I do not want to see it pulling away from me. For any reason!"

With that out of the way, he bent to press his lips

against her perspiring forehead. She tracked his feet as they retraced their steps to the scenic position at her rear. Missy could only imagine the spectacle she presented. Her back was arched like a gold winning Olympic gymnast, her naked butt an enthusiastic target just awaiting his attention.

She did not have long to wait. Without delay, four stinging blows were delivered, two per cheek. Resolute, Missy remained in place, literally unable to draw breath. Rainbow colored lights exploded behind her eyes as five more blows rained down in quick succession. She did not flinch.

After four more strokes she was gasping for air and tears were spilling down her cheeks. Wild-eyed, she braced for more.

They never came to pass.

Missy would later remember being lifted from the ironing board as if she weighed nothing. Her quivering body felt as if it were floating in his arms. Her ruptured mind drifted along behind them, basking in the warm glow of sub-space.

Eventually, she found herself curled in James' lap. His strong arms encircled her, holding her close. She laid her head against his shoulder in a mixture of nervous exhaustion and utter contentment. She inhaled the comforting scent of him, idly wondering if the tremors she was experiencing would ever pass.

Missy hoped not…

Chapter 15

James pressed his snifter of cognac to her lips, urging her to drink. Swallowing, she gagged on the strong liquor. He felt her body spasm in his lap and tightened his arms around her protectively. Again, she laid her head against his chest, right above his heart. A huge yawn encompassed what seemed her entire body. She shuddered, snuggling even closer against him.

Fulfilled, a smile played upon his lips. At the same time, a deep frown knitted his brow. The feelings this waif of a girl triggered within him were nothing short of extraordinary. They demanded a level of intimacy and personal responsibility that would be daunting to most men.

James, however, was not most men. He relished the opportunity. Yes, he could have concluded her discipline as originally designated. He could easily have administered the remaining thirteen strokes. There was no doubt that *he* would have enjoyed each and every one. But a Master worthy of the title recognizes when enough is enough before it becomes too much.

Missy had had enough.

Deep in thought, James buried his face in her now-disheveled hair. With a level of contentment he couldn't recall experiencing, he inhaled a fragrant mix of shampoo, sweat, and desire. Emanating from her in waves, it was a potent combination. James was enraptured.

Her naked, freshly spanked bottom rested squarely against the full length of his still turgid cock. The scorching heat of her penetrated the thick fabric of his jeans. His mind drifted to the delectable sight of that lovely porcelain ass raised high and straining before him. Thirteen strokes later, it was a delightful shade of crimson punctuated by pale stripes left by the well-placed slots of the spatula.

And, with that, his dick lurched. His jeans now pulled in all the wrong places. Missy moaned, stirring against him. His sudden 'expansion' would not be marginalized. James groaned. *How much control was one man expected to exercise?* James knew he was fast approaching his limit.

"It's time to get you home, little one. You have a big decision to make and little time in which to make it."

She lifted her chin, her show-stopping hazel eyes gazing up at him.

"You must decide whether you have the courage to change your life forever. Whether you are ready to accept who you've always been, and to live the life you were born to live."

"If you are brave enough to make that decision, it shall be your last. Once made, there is no turning back. For either of us."

With those portentous words, he pushed her gently from his lap onto the floor at his feet. Only the dark, viscous spot on his jeans remained. He scooped it onto his fingers and lifted them to his nose. Inhaling the intoxicating scent of sweet submission, he licked the sticky digits clean as a child might lick cookie batter from a wooden spoon.

Not for an instant did his eyes stray from hers. Missy's lifelong need was delicious as well as unmistakable. Still, it leaked freely from her unprotected body.

James instructed her to tuck her knees beneath her, then to lean back upon her heels. Preferably, with a modicum of grace. As her heels dug into the tenderized flesh of her butt cheeks, he was rewarded with a heartfelt moan.

Bending down in order to better enhance her understanding, he opened her knees as far as they would go. Exposed for his pleasure, James took full advantage of the view. He lingered, appreciating that which was splayed before him. Straightening up at last, he spoke directly into her mortified eyes.

"I know this to be your proper place, little one; on your knees at my feet. You are the woman I have long sought to complete me—the beautiful, intelligent submissive whom I feared did not exist."

"You feel it as deeply as I. If you know I speak the truth, know as well that your future will be devoid of secrets and privacy. I will know all: the woman, the person, the whore. I will be fluent in your fears and your fantasies. I will have full knowledge of every hope and every dream. Finally, I shall gorge on your deference and delight in your surrender."

James leaned down to stroke her upturned face.

"In return, my lovely, you will know a sense of belonging and accomplishment the likes of which you cannot imagine. You shall be rich in contentment, cherished and protected."

"You will love and be loved as you've never thought possible."

Chapter 16

Taking her hand, he helped her to her unsteady feet. Trying and failing to maintain her own weight, Missy leaned hard against him. James straightened her clothing as if she were a child.

He informed her that he wouldn't allow her to drive in this condition. He would call a taxi. He would also see to it that her car was returned to her in the morning. She was not to worry. That was his department.

She hung on his every word. At the moment, her entire world was reduced to him: *his* voice, *his* eyes, *his* hands. It occurred to her that she might at least attempt an independent thought. Ironically, Missy couldn't think of a single reason to do so. Even if she were able, she lacked the necessary inclination to complete the task.

She realized that she needed to use the restroom. Badly. She barely managed to croak out even that urgent request. James led her down the same hallway she'd traversed earlier in her search for the perfect spanking utensil. Her little hand tucked innocently within his was a perfect fit. It felt as though it was always meant to be there.

Missy could not account for the improbable feeling of safety that she experienced in this man's presence. He might be leading her straight to hell, and she was willingly, no— *blissfully* following. There was really no sane reason to believe that he wasn't. *Or that he hadn't already.*

Attaining the bathroom, James flipped on the light. He did not, however, release her hand. In fact, the more she attempted to extricate it, the tighter he squeezed. *How does he expect me to shut the door?* Her efforts halted as realization slowly dawned. She understood his unspoken intentions all too well. Paralyzed, Missy gaped in slack-jawed horror.

A lascivious grin spread across his chiseled features. The smile was almost, but not quite, as troublesome as the teasing words which followed.

"Devoid of secrets and privacy, little one. Have you forgotten so soon?"

The pressure to her imprisoned hand increased yet again. It was enough to re-engage the speech center of her brain, which had stalled out in disbelief. She responded almost inaudibly but without further prompting.

"No, sir. I can assure you I haven't forgotten, sir."

And there they stood. Moments ticked by in charged silence. The placid serenity which encompassed James was almost as distressing to Missy as her lewd and imminent future. He made no attempt whatsoever to disguise his obvious enjoyment.

She was convinced that James could see past the discomfiture of her features to the desperate calculations pulsing through her brain. What were the odds that she could make it home without wetting herself?

With a heavy sigh, she gave up the computation. It was well beyond her capability at this juncture, in any case. Blushing crimson, she squatted on the toilet. There was no need to pull her panties down. She'd been unencumbered of them hours ago.

Trying to imagine that she was somewhere else, *anywhere else*, was impossible. His eyes bored into hers, effectively rendering all bodily functions nonoperational. Compounding her angst, if such were possible, he moved to stand directly before her.

Still holding her hand, James opened her tightly squeezed knees as far as they would go. And then, a smidgen further. He proceeded to crouch lithely between them. Dreading her bladder would burst, Missy's eyes darted staccato. She was desperate to look anywhere, anywhere but at James. When he gently grasped her chin, her options were narrowed to one. Eyeball to eyeball it was.

The glowing pride that shone from his eyes caught her unawares. It embraced, warmed, and calmed her. A moment ago the notion of glancing at him was torturous. Now, she couldn't bear to look away.

Master...

When he began to hum gently, the dam broke. Her bladder loosed, splashing forcefully into the toilet. Missy whimpered for the duration. Yet, if she were honest, she'd admit that what she desired most in the world was for James to kiss her!

Disturbed by the insight, she managed to break eye contact at last. As she searched out the toilet paper dispenser, his next words caused the muscles in her belly to spasm.

"You may wipe today my dear, but in future, I suggest you not assume it to be your right."

Missy's hands shook visibly as she performed the intimate task under his close scrutiny. When she rose to flush, James pressed her clammy hand to his swollen crotch. No words were necessary to convey the moving effect she had on him.

Was that pride she was feeling along with his imposing manhood?

Whore!

Mercifully, there was little time to explore and

categorize her scattered emotions. The taxi honked its impatient arrival. James unbolted the heavy door which he'd locked behind them only hours before. To Missy, it represented a lifetime.

She experienced an overwhelming sense of deja vu. If she hadn't believed in previous lives, she did now. Her wish was to spend any and all future lives locked behind this very door, with this very man.

James supported most of her weight as they made their way slowly out to the cab. Once arrived, he bent her backwards across the hood, in direct view of the driver. With one leg pushed brazenly between hers, he leaned his entire weight into her. He kissed her already-opening mouth, crushing her lips with the intensity of his feelings.

Missy kissed him back with equal fervor. She kissed him with hungry lips, and the entirety of her being. Pinned beneath him, James' manhood pulsed against her all but naked crotch. The eerie sense of deja vu persisted. Everything other than his distinctly familiar presence fell away as meaningless.

When the kiss ended, Missy struggled for oxygen and composure. James helped her up, calm as a summer's breeze. He handed her into the backseat of the cab as if she were the most regal of royalty.

"You have a decision to make, my dear," he breathed into her ear before firmly shutting the door.

Shivering, she heard him instruct the driver to take good care of his precious cargo, and to keep the change. He proffered a bill large enough to deliver her into the next state.

The car began to make its way down the long driveway. Missy was tossed back against the seat cushions, numb with physical and mental exhaustion. She couldn't begin to process the astounding events of this day. A day that began as mundanely as any other, yet ended the furthest thing from!

I have a decision to make...

She couldn't help but giggle under her breath. She felt a little like Scarlett O'Hara, the southern belle from *Gone With the Wind*. Like Scarlett, she too was overwhelmed by the twists and turns of fate. Like Scarlett, she too would think about it tomorrow.

After all, tomorrow is another day...

Chapter 17

Missy had a decision to make.

Just beyond the tinted windows of the taxicab, the night lights of the city hurtled past unseen. Her immediate dilemma was to achieve a tolerable seated position. A position she could sustain for the estimated twenty minute journey home.

It might as well be forever. The cracked faux leather of the seat cushions stuck cruelly against the inflammation of her freshly paddled and very bare bottom. Any attempt at movement proved equally difficult and agonizing. She was suddenly aware of every microscopic crack in the road. With each, her unrestrained breasts pitched ludicrously hither and yon. They wobbled and jiggled unimpeded under the thin silk top.

At last, Missy managed to achieve a bearable seated position. Balanced on the edge of one fevered butt cheek, she crossed her arms to contain and conceal her unruly breasts. In her diminished mental capacity, she was convinced that her thick, fevered nipples were about to burn clean through the flimsy material.

Missy's eyes widened in distress when she accidentally brushed the mauled nipple of her left breast. Cursed with over-sensitive nipples at the best of times, she choked back the shriek that rose in her throat. Already familiar bolts of torturous sensation coursed through her body in two opposing directions: between her legs and between her ears.

Recalling how nonchalantly James reached for that distended nubbin left her breathless, chest heaving. Missy moaned with the intensity of the memory. His hand moved in what seemed like slow motion until it attained its singular objective. Once secured within his grasp, he twisted, teased, and tortured that engorged teat without respite. Yet, all the while, a courteous, almost bored smile lifted the edges of his exasperatingly distracting lips!

Appalled, Missy realized she was midway through yet another very audible moan. Swallowing it, she peeked up from beneath smudged lashes to find the cab driver smirking back. He didn't bother to disguise his drooling enjoyment as he leered at her bouncing breasts in the rear-view mirror. Missy became immediately aware of her state of disarray, specifically her lack of undergarments. She managed to maneuver herself to the furthest corner of the back seat.

Not without sacrificing what little was left of her modesty, however. Her progress was accompanied by distinctive sucking sounds. It was produced by none other than her naked ass cheeks as they stuck to, then released from, the leatherette seat. Missy bit back a yelp of pain and humiliation.

Once ensconced in the darkest corner, she melted into the shadows where prying eyes couldn't penetrate. She was grateful for the large bill that James gave the driver to deliver her safely home. With that and a little luck, she hoped to arrive unmolested as well!

The cabbie's lecherous eyes in the rear view mirror brought with them a harsh reminder of the real world. Somehow, she'd managed to disregard its existence for the bulk of this extraordinary day.

Whore!

Missy's cheeks flamed brightly enough to glow in the dark. She imagined the condemning eyes of 'polite' society were they present that evening. She envisioned their horror as the slotted spatula was mindfully chosen as the instrument of her chastisement.

Yes, Missy herself was responsible for its selection as the perfect apparatus to be applied with force against the tender flesh her own bared bottom. She further compounded her societal sins by deferentially offering the odious tool to James, hoping for his approval.

Without a doubt, however, the final 'civilized' thread was severed as she strained to raise her whore hips as high off the ironing board as possible. High enough to afford James an easier, more attainable target.

Missy perceived society's judgmental eyes as they narrowed to mere slits. She'd scrupulously avoided inviting the attention of that unforgiving entity since becoming aware of its closed-minded existence as a teen. She was sensitive to the multitude of possible repercussions, none of which were attractive. What two consenting adults did behind closed doors should be nobody's business but their own!

While these thoughts were most assuredly disturbing, more distressing was the sticky wetness which leaked incessantly from between her legs. It occurred the moment her mind touched upon the multitude of 'sinful' exploits in which she'd so eagerly participated.

And touch upon them she did. In her mind's eye, Missy observed herself being 'arranged' atop the conveniently angled ironing board. She watched as James positioned her breasts to dangle indecently from each side. She could see her arms and legs wrap around it, holding on for dear life in order to avoid a tumble. Her one mission was to not incur his displeasure. That singular focus was nothing short of liberating.

She'd been bound to that board, yet emancipated at the same time!

I have a decision to make? Missy trembled from head to toe, her lack of apparel nary to blame. The culprit was the absolute absence of choice. The decision was made on her behalf the moment she'd discovered the truth in James' riveting eyes. Her deepest secret was found out, and like Pandora's opened box, there was no going back.

Missy knew precisely where she belonged. And, to whom.

Master...

Chapter 18

With those jarring realizations, the fatigue that was nagging overtook her completely. Turning as best she could to stare out the window, her weary mind drifted to Christopher. She shed silent tears as she thought of her son and the tight bond they shared. It had always been the two of them against, well—everything. His happiness and well being was her entire world.

Just three weeks ago they'd received the long anticipated acceptance letter to Christopher's first college of choice. Was it simply a coincidence? Or, could it be what's often referred to as destiny; a concept Missy now felt merited much closer scrutiny.

While her jubilant son never suspected it, her natural maternal pride in his achievements had been fleetingly tempered. An overwhelming sense of impending loneliness gripped her. The prospect of a prolonged separation saddened her deeply. She missed him already, and he hadn't yet left.

Missy slumped in numb exhaustion, emotions too close to the surface to allocate. The cab rolled through the stop sign at the top of her street before beginning its descent. Pointing out the tiny, dimly lit house, she had the door opened and slammed shut before any further eye contact could ensue.

She felt the cabbie's eyes undressing her as she self-consciously made her way up the driveway. She couldn't even blame the poor man, overexposed as she was. The crisp, early morning air caused goose bumps to rise on her hypersensitive flesh.

Unlocking the door quietly so as not to awaken

Christopher, she freed one cramped foot at a time from her pumps. Lingering at the front entranceway, she breathed in the soothing familiarity of her surroundings. Missy froze, startled. For the second time that day, she was seized by the disturbing premonition that she didn't belong here.

Literally turning her back on the unnerving clairvoyance, she whirled to find a scribbled note on the kitchen counter. It was from her son. It read simply: *Hope you had a great time mom. Luv you.*

Missy's vision blurred. Oh, how she adored her sweet boy. In the blink of an eye, he'd grown into a fine and compassionate young man. Christopher mistakenly believed himself to be the cause of her isolated existence. He would half-jokingly lecture her that she wasn't getting any younger.

Missy sighed. She was well aware.

God, I'm going to miss him. Missy was hoping that a local college might have met his needs, but Christopher was intent on carving his own path. She couldn't be prouder if he flew to the moon without wings. Clutching the note against her heart, she stumbled down the hall to her bedroom.

Collapsing onto the bed with a groan of appreciation, she hadn't enough energy to remove the few remaining articles of tattered clothing. Her final conscious thought would have disturbed her, were she not hovering on the sweet threshold of nothingness.

Her son hoped she'd had a 'great time'? She hadn't. The reality was that she'd just experienced the most extraordinary event of her entire life!

Submissive...

Chapter 19

James sat motionless on the cedar deck that wrapped around his home. Since depositing Missy into the backseat of a taxicab and watching it depart into the night, he'd accomplished little else other than to relieve himself.

He did, however, successfully manage to top up his drink, select a Monte Cristo #1 from the humidor on his desk, and install himself into this very comfortable deck chair.

He'd attended to one other small detail, as well. He'd retrieved an ornately framed photograph of Angeline from his bedside table. Setting it cautiously atop the railing, he pulled the chair close. James then leaned back, propping his booted heels on the railing alongside it.

And, there he sat, enjoying the fragrant bouquet of damp cedar and fine cigar. The serenity of his reclined physical body belied the agitation of his churning emotions. Early on, he identified the prevalent emotion to be that of guilt. Subsequently, he'd been wiling away the hours contemplating his wife's one-dimensional countenance. James was attempting to deduce why he felt not a single modicum of remorse or longing.

Yes, he felt a natural pang of guilt for relishing another after almost three years of mourning Angeline's passing. Yet, he was the furthest thing from repentant. Truth be told, he wanted more. Much more. James had spent three long years envisioning only Angeline in those vulnerable, tortured seconds between wakefulness and sleep. Now, at long last, he hungered for another.

And hunger for Missy he did. It was an enormous admission, one he never envisioned making. With it came the adjacent jabs of conscience which he was presently sorting through. He wasn't searching for her inasmuch as he didn't presume her to exist. And then, suddenly, there she was, in as ordinary of circumstances as one could imagine: a grocery checkout line.

Dumbfounded by the foibles of fate, he understood that carrying baggage heavy enough to require a porter was the most efficient way to destroy a relationship. Including one of a Dominant/submissive flavor. It was time to leave Angeline where she belonged: in the past. It was past time to let go of the guilt and the pain and move forward.

Was he capable of such?

James realized that Missy wasn't the only one with a decision to make. Just the thought of the pure yet innocent submissive brought a wolfish smile to his face. He desired to devour the whole of her, bite by mouthwatering bite. James knew himself to be a demanding taskmaster. He wasn't arrogant enough to expect Missy to surrender the very essence of herself simply because he asked.

The grin disappeared. A man who spent much of his time wallowing in the past with a woman long dead had no right to ask in the first place.

He smiled scornfully at Angeline's ever-perfect visage. It may well be that he was squandering valuable time and energy fretting about such matters of the heart. Chances were excellent that he'd accomplished nothing this evening other than to drive Missy away – repelled by her own carnal desires. Not to mention the lengths she was willing to go to explore them.

At that very moment, she was probably racing back to the 'acceptable' world from which he'd snatched her unawares.

If so, she would be all the more determined to adapt to the ill-fitting fabric from which her previous existence was woven. Nonetheless, James closed his eyes and immersed himself in the extraordinary depths of her submissiveness.

Green tinged eyes flecked with gold, they'd nearly popped from her head as her bladder let loose its contents. Urinating into the toilet, Missy had been horror struck. He'd squatted cozily between her thighs, grinning with delight as she turned crimson from mortification.

Ahhh, life is good.

The sky began to lighten with the onset of a new day, interrupting James from his pleasant ruminations. He rose stiffly to get some much needed sleep. He was heading up a three day seminar for eighty sharp, ambitious businessmen today. Scheduled to begin in just a few short hours, he needed to be just as sharp. Sharper, in fact.

He thanked the powers that be that he instructed this particular course as often as he did. He could virtually recite it in his sleep. Truthfully, the way he was feeling at the moment, he may very well have to.

Placing Angeline's picture back in its proper place, James stripped out of his clothes. He collapsed onto his stunning four-poster, king-sized bed. One of a kind, he'd imported it from Amsterdam. He wasn't able to resist its ancient craftsmanship and charm.

Also, one never knew just when a solid, handcrafted column—or four—might come in handy!

Setting the clock a half hour earlier than was required, James mentally organized his day. The first order of business was to return Missy's car.

Chapter 20

What a difference a day makes.

Gradually peeling one gritty eyelid open at a time, Missy found herself perusing the ceiling directly above her bed. The rhythmic rotations of the fan encapsulated her complete, if minimal, consciousness.

Yawning, she stretched from head to toe. She longed to do nothing more than this for the remainder of the day. Lying prostrate in a comfy bed contemplating lazy fan blades slicing through stagnant air? To Missy, it was much more than decadent—it was prudent. She seriously questioned her capacity for more complex undertakings.

She hadn't thought to draw the blinds upon her half naked homecoming only a few short hours ago. It was the morning sunshine streaming through the bedroom window that had finally succeeded in rousing her. Now, that same brilliance served to launch her into a full-blown tizzy.

What time was it?

Bolt upright now, she ignored the pounding ache which defined her left nipple and disregarded the searing heat which was her butt. Missy turned trepidatiously towards the alarm clock. Glaring at it as thought it should have set itself, she all but sprang from the bed.

She was late. *Again.*

Yet, punctuality wasn't the only challenge she faced on this exceptional morning. Complicating matters further was the fact that she had no vehicle to transport her to her place of employment.

Almost immediately, dizzying waves of mortification engulfed her. There was no way to distort the jaw-dropping details of the previous evening. Impossible to minimize the series of events which had rendered her incapable of maneuvering her car from point A to point B.

Or herself, for that matter.

Missy didn't have the age-old luxury of blaming her bad behavior on alcohol. She hadn't a single drink, never mind one too many. On the other hand, she was seriously reevaluating the accepted definition of 'bad'. Blushing, she admitted that James made her feel anything and everything *except* bad. *If that was bad, it felt very, very good!*

Missy forced her lagging mind back to the here and now. She wracked her brains for a solution to the issue of transportation and her lack thereof. She couldn't call James', she'd left his business card in the car. In any case, what remained of it was probably little more than a crumpled, sweat stained mess.

Not that it mattered. Sighing, she accepted her train of thought was getting her nowhere fast. Even if the card were available to her, she would never have the nerve to actually call. There was no use standing here debating it further. She would just grab a cab and pay for her trespasses.

With that decided, a determined Missy relegated the events of the past fourteen hours to the status of anomaly. Yes, simply a glitch in the fabric of the universe. A glitch that just happened to send bolts of white light through her mind and waves of desire through her body!

Missy veered away from that truth, concentrating instead on rummaging drawers and closets. She automatically selected only black garments, as mandated by Ebony&Ivory's strict dress code. Her mind refused to cooperate despite the time. At the moment, it was busy exploring the animalistic passion she felt towards a rare and mysterious man.

Animalistic didn't begin to define it. She was mortified by the lengths she'd been willing to go in order to convey her desire to James. Not to mention the depths she'd been eager to plunge. It horrified her to imagine what more she might have been capable of, given time.

A shower was mandatory. No matter that it would further delay her already overdue departure. She felt like the proverbial horse, ridden hard and put away wet. It would never do to show up at one of the most exclusive boutiques in the city stinking like a common whore.

With a shocking sense of arrogance, Missy cinched her shoulders back.

This whore was far from common!

Chapter 21

There was precious little time for meandering thoughts. Missy was functioning under the treacherous combination of too little sleep and an excess of sensory stimuli. This dangerous duo made it imperative to concentrate only on the most immediate concerns.

First and foremost she needed to get her rosy red ass to work. Second, she needed to find an innovative method of keeping it moving and productive for what already seemed like an endless day.

She saved time by washing, brushing, and relieving herself in the shower. She then proceeded to lose as much time, or more, by rolling her discarded clothing into a ball and pressing them to her face. Missy inhaled as deeply as she could. Twice. His scent was tangible and mingled with her own.

If she was her boss, she'd have fired her own butt long ago. Instead, Teresa would put her arm around Missy's shoulders. She would whisper in her ear that she hadn't gotten to where she was by cutting off her nose to spite her face. Missy was her most trusted and productive employee, if not the most punctual. *The clientele simply adore you, dah-ling!*

Once, Teresa went so far as to adjust Missy's start time —a noble attempt which failed miserably. Somehow, she managed to maintained her normal twenty to thirty minute deferral. She may be loyal and dependable, but her internal clock was irreparably out of sync with that which the rest of the world adhered.

Long ago, she'd given up wearing a watch. The only

time she ever paid attention to it was when it chafed at her wrist. Much like the bra she was attempting to fasten was chafing at her nipples. The left nipple in particular. Missy endured the irritation with more than a small measure of exasperation. She marveled at how a single evening with a mysterious, charismatic man could disrupt a lifetime of enforced convention.

She multi-tasked out of habit and desperation, not mental acuity. She managed to twist her hair into some semblance of a knot, apply a dab of lip gloss, and call a cab. As she gave her address to the dispatcher, she closed her burning eyes. Missy sent up a silent prayer that it wouldn't be the same driver from just a few short hours before. *I'd rather die on the spot than crawl into the backseat of that cab to die of shame!*

Hurrying to the kitchen, she reheated a to-go mug of day old coffee, and was grateful for it. She usually brewed fresh, of course. But, that was on those more conventional mornings when extraordinary, life-altering events hadn't transpire the evening before.

She heard Christopher already tap-tap-tapping away, and figured he must be spreading the news of his college acceptance. She had long worried about the momentous cost of tuition, and they both did what they could to offset the inevitable. While student loans were already in the works, Christopher had been delivering pizza since the day he passed his driver's exam. With monumental self-discipline, he banked any and all tips.

Missy, too, saved whatever meager remnants her paycheck allowed. Sadly, all too often it was Christopher who accounted for the lion's share. His father would be making his usual contribution towards his son's bright future: nothing! Quite the contrary, Luke was a constant drain on their meager resources.

His list of priorities was short and far from sweet. Pornography and alcohol, in any order. Next would be accruing enough money to indulge the former two. The end. The revered list excluded all children, first and foremost his own.

Not that Luke hadn't been crystal clear regarding his disdain for children. He had. Unfortunately, Missy was allergic to oral contraceptives and Luke was allergic to responsibility. Two small details that slipped his usually inebriated mind. After his favorite watering holes closed, he would come home slobbering drunk and horny. There was no reasoning with him.

Thankfully, he lost all interest in her when she 'accidentally' became pregnant. His only lingering attraction to Missy revolved around her impressive culinary skills. Luke had no qualms whatsoever about sitting down shirtless at the dinner table with marks from other women on his back.

She left him shortly after Christopher was born, and, of course, blamed herself. While she'd believed herself in love with him when they married, she couldn't say for certain if she ever truly had. She suspected that she'd married him to prove to herself and the world that she was 'normal'.

Once, heart pounding, Missy offered to share a fantasy with her new husband. She'd prayed he might find her 'uniqueness' of some small interest, and perhaps even reciprocate with a fantasy of his own.

Instead, his response shattered her. Luke informed her that he didn't have fantasies. Further, he wasn't the least bit interested in hers. He served only to reinforce what she long suspected: she was far from normal.

Submissive...

The taboo topic was never raised again. The newlyweds engaged in silent, passionless sex. They did not make love. The only sounds were Luke's guttural grunts as he sawed into her with his eyes squeezed shut. His position of choice was missionary. He never inquired as to hers.

Not surprisingly, he never excited Missy in the bedroom. Not even at the apex of his short-lived prime. Instead, she would masturbate to the same wicked fantasies of Dominance and submission that had always plagued her. When she'd finally had enough of his abuse and left, he used the occasion as just another excuse to get drunk and mean.

Drunker and meaner. Nothing had changed to this day.

Christopher didn't look up from the computer when Missy tapped and poked her head in. Best he not see the naked guilt which constituted her expression in any case. Yes, she wished she'd provided him an actual father instead of just a sperm donor. But Luke gave her Christopher, and for that she would be forever grateful.

Missy blew her son a quick kiss, said good morning and goodbye in the same breath, and turned to leave. Head down, he asked, "How was your date last night, mom?"

Before she could even open her mouth the cab beep-beeped its arrival. Thankfully, she'd been rescued from a simple question to which the answer would be far more complex. To cover her consternation, she scolded him, teasing that he was worse than a dog with a bone.

At the sound of the now blaring horn, Christopher at last looked up from the computer. Missy avoided the quizzical glance he shot her way. With a nervous smile, she withdrew from the room and closed the door behind her.

Chapter 22

Grabbing her purse and sweater, Missy sprinted from the house. She skidded to an unexpected halt on the front porch, confused. The puzzlement that clouded her features was soon replaced by delighted comprehension. Making her way around to the driver's side of the taxi, she leaned towards the opened window and explained the sudden change of plan.

Grateful to see an unfamiliar face behind the wheel, she dug a five dollar bill from her purse. Proffering it, she apologized, thanking him for his trouble. She saw the annoyance in his eyes dissipate and he smiled back. While he accepted the outstretched bill, he drove away apologizing for doing so.

Turning, she took a few tentative steps in the direction of her car. There it sat, smack in the middle of the driveway, as if by magic. It hadn't sparkled like that since it was new. Well, new to her. Missy's heart melted and unexpected tears blurred her bloodshot eyes.

Thankfully, it was no longer necessary to navigate the sticky logistics of retrieving her vehicle. That task had weighed arduous on her mind. Her heart palpitated at the very notion of seeing James. There was only one word for the effect he has on her mind and body.

Submissive...

Shaking her head in disbelief, Missy climbed into the driver's seat. A sweet floral aroma enveloped her, calming her frayed nerves. Missy scanned the newly-detailed interior for keys. No luck. They weren't in the ignition or anywhere else that she could see. What she did discover, however, caused her heart to cease palpitating in her chest and begin to thump wildly in her ears.

On the passenger seat was a single, long-stemmed red rose, a small box, and a note. Picking up the rose, she accidentally pricked her thumb on a thorn. Mesmerized as a droplet of blood sprang forth, she inhaled from the fragrant bloom of the identical hue.

Licking at the blood to stem the flow, Missy opened the box. An involuntary gasp escaped her. Instead of the keys she expected to find, she discovered a beautiful silver choker with a tiny circlet pendant. The filament was so delicate, it seemed an intermittent shimmer against her throat. The elegant pendant rested in the notch where her collar bones met.

She couldn't stop touching it. Looking at herself in the rear-view mirror, she paid no mind to the late hour or the repercussions she would suffer as a result. Her wide grin compared in brilliance with that of the iridescent chain. She managed to drag her eyes away from it, but only to read the enclosed note from her Master.

Master? Struck dumb by the word she chose to describe him, Missy focused instead on the missive. Her hand trembled as she reached for it. "Good morning, little one. I trust you slept well, if not long. I appreciate your entrusting me with your address and phone number, not to mention your luscious mind and body. Given time, you shall come to realize that I am worthy of such trust. And given trust, you will come to surrender considerably more to me. In fact you shall surrender heart, mind, body and soul. In turn, I shall never forsake such precious gifts. The keys are under your seat, my lovely—which I imagine is still burning with memories of me."

It was signed simply 'James'. Missy quite literally panted

like a bitch in heat as she read, then re-read his words. Today, her choice of underwear was made of *much* sturdier stuff than the flimsy ones of yesterday. Placing the now blood smeared note aside, she located the keys, started the engine, and backed out of the driveway.

Missy sighed. It was apparent that even these panties offered precious little protection against his onslaught.

Master...

Chapter 23

Pulling into an open space in the employee parking area of Boutique Ebony&Ivory, Missy turned off the engine. Drawing several deep breaths, she attempted to quell her apprehension. She was well over an hour late. Although she had texted the extent of her inexcusable tardiness, she exceeded even that estimation. She did not relish facing Teresa's displeasure, however justified.

She was scrambling from the Infinity when she remembered to remove the chain from around her neck. She did so reluctantly, feeling naked without it. Nonetheless, she was in buckets of trouble already.

It was strict policy that employees not wear their own jewelry to work. This statute precluded any awkward requests from admiring customers who might wish to purchase an identical piece. Not that any jewelry she owned would inspire the admiration of the shop's uber-wealthy clientele.

They were, however, encouraged to display pieces from the shop's own exclusive collections. There were cases brimming with sparkling jewels ranging from brooches and bracelets to cocktail rings and tiaras. Pieces were signed out at the beginning of a shift and back in at the conclusion—always under the watchful eye of Teresa.

While undeniably a highlight for the employee, this brilliant strategy was designed with the clientele and the bottom line in mind. It provided an up-close-and-personal view of some spectacular baubles that might otherwise have been overlooked. It was a win-win marketing ploy which proved highly profitable.

Missy hurried through the breathtaking double doors

of the boutique's entryway. They opened before her as though admitting a princess to the king's chambers. She never failed to be struck by the sheer extravagance of these enormous cut-glass doors. Perilously, they captivated the attention of anyone driving down the narrow street. As was their function, of course.

The left was engraved with a sensual, cursive 'E', the right with the matching 'I'. Both sparkled as if anointed with fairy dust. They were meticulously polished thrice daily, usually by Missy herself. She kept her head down and headed straight for the staff room. She thanked the powers that be that today was Wednesday, one of the quietest days of the week.

As she stashed her purse and sweater, she glanced at the schedule to see who was working. Relief washed over her when she saw that it was Stephanie and only Stephanie. A quick check in the mirror and within seconds, she was on the floor searching out Teresa. Best to get this over with sooner rather than later. Fortunately, the shop was devoid of customers.

Adding to her dismay, she located Teresa behind the massive front desk. She was up to her knees in a task that was no doubt intended for Missy. An enormous delivery of summer inventory arrived that morning. It was priority one to get it separated, counted, hung, steamed, sized, priced – and onto the floor. The first rule of retail is that nothing sells sitting in a box.

"Teresa, I can't begin to tell you how sorry I am. There's no excuse for it, and I won't insult you any further by offering one. I deserve any disciplinary action you see fit."

Chapter 24

Teresa, drowning in a sea of rumpled Vera Wang frocks, turned to face her. Frustration and disappointment were written all over her face. If it were possible, Missy felt worse still. She very much respected her boss. Over the years they'd developed a warm relationship.

Teresa usually treated her more like a daughter than an employee. She was very concerned about her raising a son alone. She often chided Missy for not being more receptive to the ardent advances of men who would make her life easier. Much like Christopher, one of Teresa's favorite lines was, *"After all, darling, none of us are getting any younger, now are we?"* Missy sighed. Teresa wasn't feeling terribly maternal at the moment.

"We'll discuss this in my office."

She barely ground out the words before turning her back on Missy and beckoning to Stephanie, the only other employee in the shop. She left Stephanie with instructions to continue where she'd left off and to call if she required assistance. She then turned on her heel, marched rigidly to her office, swung open the door, and stepped aside. There was just enough room for Missy to squeeze by.

Teresa not only closed the office door behind them, she locked it. Missy knew things were about to go very badly. Just how badly was yet to be seen.

"You are making my job very difficult, Missy Miss, and this time, you better have a damned good explanation!"

She paused for breath, her annoyance unrestrained.

"Your habit of getting to work late every day has become a bit of a company joke. Everyone knows that you more than make up for it in sales and overtime. *But this?*"

Teresa and her brother Michael had inherited the boutique from their mother. The entrepreneurial matriarch had suffered a massive coronary just four months previous to Missy being hired. It was hard to believe that was over seven years ago.

Michael enjoyed a thriving career as a stock broker and cared not one whit for women's fashion. Nor women, for that matter. The only trends that interested him were financial in nature. It fell to his grieving sister to ensure that their mother's passion survived her passing.

The bawdy Teresa admitted only to being 'somewhere' in her forties. She was shockingly tall and shockingly thin. Her crowning glory was a mass of shockingly overly-processed platinum blonde hair. As it turned out, she was also blessed with a shockingly good eye for style and a razor sharp mind for business. Her ideas were innovative and fresh. The boutique not only survived, it flourished.

She hadn't budged since she began reading Missy the riot act. She stood as though blocking the locked office door, hands on hips. Teresa was well and truly pissed.

"This is downright disrespectful!"

Upon hearing those words, the tears that had been threatening spilled over unchecked. Words tumbled from Missy's mouth, also unchecked.

"Oh, Teresa, can you ever forgive me? I truly couldn't be sorrier and you have my word that it will never happen again. It's just that I met this strange man yesterday and didn't get home until almost four in the morning and then I fell asleep without setting the alarm and my car wasn't there when I woke up, and..."

Her mouth snapped shut the instant she noticed the astonishment spreading across Teresa's face. *What am I saying?* She rarely if ever opened up about her personal life. Yet, here she was crying like a baby and spilling her guts all over her boss's ornate mahogany desk!

Mortified, she hung her head to await the inevitable...

Chapter 25

"You met a man? As in a living breathing male?"

At last, Teresa moved from the door and took a seat behind her desk. She rolled her plush leather chair up close to Missy's, who sat desolate, bracing for the worst.

Ignoring the defeated expression on Missy's drawn face, Teresa challenged her.

"Had I known yesterday that you had a date, I'd have made damn sure you were properly dressed for the occasion!"

There was no way to discern whether Teresa was less, or more, pissed off. Missy would have been delighted to share with her boss the historic tidings of a rare date. Had there in fact been one.

She glanced up, amazed to find Teresa sporting a grin the Cheshire Cat would envy. Dumbfounded by the one hundred and eighty degree turn in mood and tone, Missy swiped at the tears staining her cheeks. She was unable to resist Teresa's infectious enthusiasm, and offered a small smile of gratitude in return.

"Can you forgive me Teresa? I'll work overtime for a week straight."

She was cut her off.

"Well, my dear, I'll definitely take you up on that overtime. At the moment, however, I'm far more interested in hearing all about this new man. So? Do tell!"

Missy sighed in order to buy time. She scrambled to think of what she could tell this kind woman who cared so much about her well-being. While she loathed being dishonest, she certainly wasn't about to tell her the truth, the whole truth, and nothing but the truth.

She could just imagine the look on Teresa's face as she recounted the finer points of her so-called date. It wouldn't be long before her expression changed from captivated to disgusted. *Well, it's like this don't ya see, Teresa. I went from meeting a complete stranger in a grocery store to spreading my legs on his toilet in order for him to better observe my urinating. And, oh yes, did I mention that it was the most incredible experience of my entire life?*

She didn't want to give poor Teresa a coronary. Wasn't it enough that one of them was already suffering from heart palpitations and light-headedness? Missy managed to utter two garbled words before the shrill buzz of the intercom interjected. It was Stephanie, ringing for reinforcements. There were too many customers to manage by herself.

Missy was quite literally saved by the bell. As they exited the office, she wondered if Teresa noticed her lips moving in a silent prayer of gratitude. She sighed with relief even as turmoil continued to rage within.

Persons of an alternative nature tended towards extreme privacy, often verging on paranoia. After all, they sustained within themselves a socially unsustainable secret. Like any subculture, they were terrified to emerge from their proverbial closets. Historically, the backlash towards those who dared to deviate from the norm tended to be a bit of a bitch.

Thus far, Missy and her secret had survived that over-crowded, claustrophobic cubbyhole. On the other hand, the accompanying psychological effects were becoming a source of concern. Guarding a secret takes its inevitable toll. The trade-off is burdensome, detrimental to both health and quality of life.

Why couldn't people just mind their own business?

In short order, each of the three customers was provided the personalized, patient, and deferential service that was expected from the staff at Boutique Ebony&Ivory. Once the coast was clear, Missy bear-hugged a surprised but laughing Stephanie. Steph was her friend and favorite co-worker, even if they did come from completely opposite sides of the tracks.

She looked to be about twenty years Missy's senior, but looks could be deceiving. The age of plastic surgery made it virtually impossible to gauge with any degree of accuracy. Missy was well aware that the shops clientele indulged as much in tucking, sucking and *enhancing* as they did designer shoes and bags. In any case, Stephanie was a beautiful person from the inside out. She embodied an endearing combination of easy laughter, sparkling green eyes, and a compassionate soul.

She worked simply because she got bored sitting at home. She certainly didn't need the money. Steph was married to George T. Weatherly, one of the most respected judges in the state, if not the country. She traveled in the same social circles as many of the highfalutin' customers she attended to so graciously. While the Weatherly's net worth may not compare with some in their social sphere, the respect her husband garnered opened doors that would have remained closed otherwise.

Missy wondered if it might also have a little something to do with his wife's sophisticated bearing and sweet disposition. In any case, she had grown very fond of Stephanie, and she knew the feelings were mutual. Steph's hysterical insight into the hallowed lives of the *uppity* class, as she called them, kept Missy in stitches and made long hours fly.

Taking over the task of processing the wrinkled Vera Wang frocks, she again thanked her lucky stars for the small mercies granted her. Working with Stephanie on the slowest day of the week and Teresa's unexpected clemency were definitely blessings that deserved to be counted.

Particularly on this grueling day. A day she wasn't at all convinced she could survive without an extended nap. A day that followed a night like no other.

Without skipping a beat, her thoughts made a beeline for James. Shaking her head in a hopeless attempt to banish him from her mind, she scooped up an armful of Vera. She left Stephanie to mind the shop while she went to the back to begin steaming the wrinkles away.

Missy chuckled to herself. If only she could steam the wrinkles from her own treacherous nature as easily.

Submissive...

Chapter 26

At the moment, Teresa remained shut away in her office. But, Missy knew it was only a matter of time before her very direct line of questioning would resume. Teresa was a die-hard romantic who couldn't resist a good piece of gossip. Hoping it might somehow slip her mind was an exercise in futility.

It was seven years since Teresa took a giant leap of faith and hired Missy straight off the street. In all those years, she'd never heard a whisper about a man in Missy's life. Other than her son, Christopher, of course. And, all too often, his deadbeat father.

Missy steadfastly declined her well-meaning boss's countless attempts to set her up. That is, with one disastrous exception. When Teresa refused to take no for an answer, Missy hadn't the heart, nor the stamina, to rebuff her yet again.

After all, Ethan Montgomery III was rich, rich, *rich!* As a wealthy and eligible bachelor, he was pursued by every ambitious debutante in town. Yet, for some reason Missy couldn't fathom, Ethan remained fascinated with her.

Teresa had all but dragged her into the samples closet. The 'closet' was a hermetically sealed, temperature controlled vault boasting security that would cause the White House to turn green with envy. It was here that a veritable ocean of eye-popping trends for the upcoming season were secreted. When they'd finally emerged, Missy felt like a cross between a Stepford Wife and Cinderella.

She had to admit, she felt pretty princess-y. Dressed in a stunning white-on-black Stella McCartney cocktail dress matched with scarlet Christian Louboutin heels, she was breathtaking. Admiring herself in the three-piece mirror, she'd begun to feel decidedly more optimistic about the possibilities of the upcoming evening. Maybe Teresa was right. Maybe she should date more often.

The ensemble was completed with a scarlet Louis Vuitton clutch and sexy chandelier earrings. Missy was teetering stylishly around in no time. The five inch heels would take some practice, of that there was no question.

Long story short, to call the evening abominable would be a compliment. There could be no denying that Ethan was handsome in the traditional tall and dark sense. He was also tailored to within an inch of his life. Unfortunately, she was forced to spend most of the evening deflecting his diamond-laden, manicured hands that kept wandering to her side of the table.

Not only that, her eyes watered from holding her breath. There was an almost visible cloud of hybrid cologne that enveloped him. Images of Charlie Brown's Pigpen danced through her oxygen depleted head. Dabbing at her mascara, she did her best to feign interest in Ethan's multinational financial exploits. To Missy, they were two things: grandiose and boring.

Not once did he pause to inquire as to herself or her life. It was only out of respect for her boss that she didn't run screaming from the swanky restaurant, five inch heels be damned. She did manage to escape before dessert, citing a terrible headache. It wasn't a lie.

Never again did Teresa attempt to arrange a date on her behalf. Nonetheless, Missy knew how much she cared, and felt she owed her at least some sort of explanation today.

What that explanation might consist of, she had no idea.

She almost giggled when a line from *I Love Lucy* popped randomly into her head. It was one of her favorite shows on cable. No matter that it had seen its heyday before she was born. *Like Lucy, I'm gonna have some 'splainin' to do.*

A lot of 'splainin', in fact.

Existing in a pea-soupy fog, Missy had no clear concept of how she survived the remainder of the day. She evaded Teresa by serving the occasional customer or hiding in the back processing merchandise.

Normally over the lunch hour, she would be ensconced in the staffroom partaking of a bag lunch. However, there'd been precious little time for anything resembling normal that morning. Her tummy growled its displeasure. She ignored it and kept busy.

She was elated when there were only a couple of hours left in this most arduous of days. It was then she heard the majestic door chimes which so dramatically announced the arrival of a customer. Knowing that Steph was up front, she completed the last batch of steaming. As she gathered the dresses up to get them on the floor, she almost collided with a very pale Stephanie, who was rushing to the back to fetch her.

"What's wrong, Steph? You look as if you've seen a ghost!"

Her friend was just about bouncing out of her shoes with excitement. Words tumbled from her mouth.

"James Colton is here and he's asking for *you*! Do you know who James Colton is? He plays golf with George but I haven't seen him in years!"

James Colton? Here? Missy mouthed the words. Her face drained of color while Stephanie's flushed pink. One was succumbing to shock while the other was recovering. Recognizing the formal name only from his business card, Missy threw the dresses in Stephanie's general direction.

She stumbled from the back of the boutique as if suddenly afflicted with a serious case of vertigo. She'd almost convinced herself that she would never see this man again. The very idea had left her feeling queasy.

Attempting to regain a modicum of balance and some semblance of composure, she lingered at the threshold of the main showroom. Her eyes locked upon James as if laser focused.

The sight of him selecting frilly items from the intimates section did nothing to facilitate Missy's equilibrium...

Chapter 27

James sensed her presence, glancing up to meet her startled eyes. Smiling, he spoke as though they were the only two people in the world.

"Come to me, little one."

Missy obeyed immediately. Pleased, he noted the absence of hesitation as she moved towards him in an almost hypnotic-like state. Coming to a graceful halt before him, her shoulders straightened and her eyes lowered. Delighted, James reached out and stroked her cheek. His mood changed, however, when he noticed her neck. For some reason, it was bereft of the silver choker.

Before he could request an explanation, a commotion erupted. Stephanie and Teresa emerged as one from Teresa's office, chittering like gossiping schoolgirls. It was clear that his arrival had been trumpeted to the loftiest of heights.

"James, it's so good to see you. It's been far too long."

Teresa gushed as she kiss-kissed him on both cheeks. Observing, one might assume they were standing in the shadow of the Eiffel Tower itself. James could practically see Teresa's sharp mind working as her eyes darted between him and Missy. His eyes crinkled in amusement when she turned directly to Missy, a knowing look on her face.

"Mr. Colton's the reason you were later than usual this morning? He's the date you spoke of, isn't he? Hmmm..."

It struck James as against Missy's nature to discuss their unforeseen and extremely intimate encounter with anyone. That said, it intrigued him to observe the array of emotions that paraded across her flushed face. It was clear that poker would not be a diversion at which she would excel. At long last, she responded to Teresa's pointed question.

"Yes, ma'am. Mr. Colton's the unexpected 'date' I mentioned."

Teresa almost hooted. Plucking the delicate garments that he'd selected from his arms, she unceremoniously deposited them into Missy's. Directing her to place them in one of the private dressing room, she linked her arm through James' and gave him her most dazzling smile.

"Surely you have time for a nice glass of wine and a chat? I'd so love to catch up."

He'd barely nodded his assent before Teresa swept him off in the direction of her office. All that remained in their wake was a whiff of his cologne and the sound of her tinkling laughter.

And Missy's inaudible squeals of horror.

Groaning under the almost unbearable weight of the few feminine frillies she was suddenly encumbered with, Missy moved towards the private dressing rooms. Boutique Ebony&Ivory catered to the desires of wealthy women. Yet, their commitment to providing the complete 'European experience' led to some noteworthy practices. One example was displaying irresistible baubles utilizing as ebony-clad sales staff as mobile backdrops.

Another? These two richly appointed private rooms. On Monday through Wednesday evenings, men were encouraged to come in to shop for their mothers, secretaries, wives and/or mistresses.

Invited to relax on plush sofas, they were offered an array of refreshments. This included the option of a glass of wine or a flute of champagne. Soft classical music was piped in through a multitude of unobtrusive speakers. The crème de la crème of fashion publications were conspicuously displayed throughout both cozy enclaves.

The most flattering lighting available illuminated a small, slightly elevated platform. This mini-stage was surrounded by a semicircle of floor to ceiling smoked mirrors. It was upon this podium that a staff member would model the garments which the gentleman had selected.

There were two restrictions attached to this pair of private rooms. They were written in stone, no exceptions. The first concerned the door. It remained open. Period. The second prohibited the modeling of undergarments or lingerie. Failure to adhere to either policy would result in the immediate termination of the offending staff member. The man would be escorted from the premises and banned.

Teresa meant business, excuse the pun.

That she'd so casually instructed her to place these undergarments in a private dressing room alarmed Missy almost as much as James' unexpected arrival. Almost as much as watching the two of them stroll off arm-in-arm, to discuss who-knew-what!

With blatant disregard, Teresa was breaking one of her two hard-and-fast rules. Missy could only assume that the second was soon to follow. She grappled with James' obvious familiarity with the boutique. Not to mention her boss's over-the-top and unprofessional behavior.

Entering the inner sanctum, Missy located the cleverly hidden change room. It was virtually invisible behind the middle expanse of mirror that encircled the dais. As she hung the delicates on separate antique brass hooks, she was able to scrutinize the lingerie for the first time. Her breath caught in her throat.

There was no question as to his exquisite taste. Every article of clothing in Boutique Ebony&Ivory was black, white, or a combination thereof. The pricey accessories, however, came in every shade imaginable. Colorful hats, belts, shoes, bags, scarves—and lingerie—made for an eye-catching contrast against the checkerboard backdrop.

The traditional Victorian La Perla corset James selected was of a sleek virginal white, as were the matching ruffled panties. The shortie negligee was of the softest pink hue imaginable, so sheer as to almost trick the eye as to its very existence. The matching bra and thong panties were of a slightly darker shade. Missy was thankful for that small mercy, at least.

Lingerie was a luxury that Missy was never able to indulge. Now, the thought of parading around half naked in front of James was not something she savored. Particularly not at her place of employment!

Yet, had Missy the ability to see into her immediate future, she would agree that parading around half naked was the least of her concerns...

Chapter 28

"I envision you in nothing other than cuffs, collars, and clamps, my dear. Perhaps a nice ball gag or butt plug to complete the ensemble."

James relaxed on the sofa, leaning back with legs splayed wide. Seemingly with all the time in the world, he gnawed on his favorite cigar and sipped at the dregs of a so-so glass of chardonnay.

The door was firmly closed, courtesy of Teresa herself. But not until she'd reminded James three times to use the intercom at his elbow if he should require anything. *Anything at all, James.*

Missy stood before him on the well lit stage. From his vantage point, he could literally see the goose bumps as they rose on her flesh.

"But alas, this quaint little shop doesn't offer such charming accoutrements, so we shall have to make do. Shan't we, my delightful little whore?"

Although it proved necessary to repeat the query, James' patience was rewarded. Her words were almost inaudible.

"Yes, sir...Make do sir."

"Good girl! Now, let's begin with the pink, shall we?"

It wasn't a question and she didn't need telling twice. Before long the changing room door opened, if only a crack. Missy's beautiful, if stricken face peeked out.

"Don't make me wait, girl!"

James snapped the words at her. Their effect was precisely as he'd expected. She didn't hesitate one second further. Missy scurried from the change room to stand in the middle of the dais. Self-conscious, she wrapped her arms around herself. James' cock stiffened at the sight of her delectable, albeit useless attempts to cover herself. She was stunning in her innocence.

The negligee wasn't half bad either.

"Be still and stand straight, girl. Arms at your sides, shoulders back, breasts up and out. Surely you can't have forgotten so quickly? I can see you're going to be labor intensive, what with having to tell you everything twice."

The red of her cheeks clashed markedly with the pink of her negligee. Nonetheless, she placed her rigid arms by her sides, pressing her shoulders back in the exaggerated manner he preferred.

"What is *that?*"

James pointed unwaveringly at the offending object until Missy's mouth fell open in comprehension.

"Do you mean...the bra?"

He leaned forward, enunciating each syllable, disallowing for any future miscommunication.

"What did we discuss about your wearing a brassiere in my presence? Have you forgotten that conversation as well? Clearly, I ought to have meted out the entirety of your well earned punishment. The leniency I displayed has gone unappreciated, if not utterly disregarded."

He looked her straight in the eye.

"I shan't make that mistake again, rest assured, my dear."

She was tearing the poor excuse for a bra off before his first sentence was completed. Words tripped over themselves in her haste to assure him that she remembered very well, indeed.

"Forgive me, sir. It came with the negligee. I just assumed..."

To accommodate his expanding cock, James was forced to lean back. Long legs extended, he splayed them flagrantly. Taking his time, he examined Missy from head to toe. She began to squirm under the close scrutiny. Yet, as quickly as the fidgeting began, it ceased. He hadn't needed to remind her.

Perfect.

"Walk towards me, my lovely. And please, put a spring in your gait. I want to watch your tits bounce as you approach."

The sharp intake of her breath served to bring a contented smile to his face. It also made even the reclined position intolerable for his growing manhood. As she took her first unsteady and most assuredly bouncy steps in his direction, James reached down and undid his pants. He pulled out not only his distended cock, but his heavy balls as well!

He seriously wondered if Missy might faint. Her eyes were huge, glued spellbound to his exposed and engorged genitalia. He admonished her to not keep him waiting a second time. He warned her that his patience did not extend as far as his cock. He'd have no compunction whatsoever in putting her over his knee if she insisted.

"And, please remember to keep those beautiful breasts bouncing. There's my good girl."

Chapter 29

Coming to a graceful halt between his knees, Missy awaited his next whim. She stood in the exaggerated posture that James favored: back arched, breasts straining against the gauzy material of the negligee. She had naught to ponder other than pleasing him.

As panic stricken as she'd been as the afternoon's events unfolded, she could not deny the pervasive sense of well being that now encompassed her. James succeeded in eliciting emotions she'd never experienced nor imagined.

Master…

Without fully grasping why, Missy knew she could entrust this unique man with her life. She understood that the connection they shared went far deeper than physical attraction. She also perceived that neither would ever feel whole again without the other. She knew these things as surely as she loved her son and as deeply as she missed her parents.

It was as if James were reading her thoughts.

"Know that you are always safest in your Master's arms and at your Master's feet, little one."

His loving tone changed not one iota.

"Now, please turn away from me, bend from the hip, and reach for your ankles."

Bend over and grab her ankles? No one had ever spoken to Missy in such a manner. She knew unequivocally that had anyone tried, they'd have been slapped silly. Why was it then, that for this one man, she would put her dignity second to his pleasure and approval? And by doing so, experience what could only be described as glowing pride?

Submissive...

Her priority was simply whichever task he assigned. And, so it was that she obeyed without hesitation. Bending, Missy grabbed her ankles, which in turn caused her butt cheeks to spread. They were now wantonly undulating in James' face. She was grateful, at least, that he couldn't see the scorching fire that was her face.

His raucous laughter only intensified the burn.

"However shall we explain to Teresa your slimy cunt juice ruining a perfectly good pair of her panties, whore? Your undisciplined hole is starting to ooze at the very thought of me, isn't it?"

Missy was in no position to disagree. Her response was truthful, if breathless.

"Yes, sir, it is."

"Why am I not the least bit surprised?"

James chuckled. At the same time, he fingered the quickly expanding wet spot. Shifting his focus, he stuffed the satiny material of the panties between her accommodating ass cheeks.

Missy's face burned hotter still. She yelped aloud when he pressed his fingers into the faded marks left by the spatula. She did not pull away, however. Nor did she leave go of her ankles.

"Mmmm, very nice, little one. You take a spanking exquisitely. I am pleased."

And, just like that—so was Missy.

James instructed her to turn towards him and kneel. She couldn't obey fast enough. Suddenly, he grabbed her by the back of the hair, pulling her forward until her entire face was buried deep in his ball sac. She was too stunned to offer resistance.

"This is your reward for being an obedient whore. What do you say?"

"Hank ou ery uch, Hir."

Missy knew her destiny was sealed..

Chapter 30

While the sensation of her breath warming his scrotum was quite enjoyable, the view was equally scrumptious. With Missy's auburn locks in his grasp, her forehead pressed snug against the base of his unyielding cock. James afforded her very little wiggle room.

Her lips and nose were quite literally buried in his balls. He was delighted when he detected them pressing deeper still.

"That's it, my lovely. You know exactly where you belong, don't you?"

He wasn't quite finished.

"You may suckle as you wish, pet."

And with that blasphemous statement, he awaited the inevitable. Societal expectations are ingrained from an early age. James knew that it was only a matter of Missy grasping the meaning of his forbidden words before she revolted against them. At last, he heard her grunt in shocked comprehension. When she attempted to jerk her head away, he disallowed it, holding firm.

"Easy now, little one. Your Master is the only judge you need concern yourself with now. You have my permission to be who you are and who you've always been: a magnificent, submissive woman!"

"In fact, I insist on it, and I suggest you not test my patience further."

With his reassuring words, all remaining doubt fell away. Trusting in him, her ragged breathing adapted to the restrictions presented. Audibly, it slowed and strengthened. The pressure of his hand entangled in her hair was somehow comforting.

Inhaling through her nostrils, she recognized his primal scent in the depths of her soul. Hungry for him, her lips burrowed into his balls, lost in the freedom granted her at this singular man's feet. She was stunned when it dawned on her that the guttural slurping and lapping sounds she heard in the distance were, in fact, coming from deep within her own throat.

Missy functioned on instinct alone. The insistent guidance of his hand was a dual edged sword. It augmented her need to please him *and* her mortification. For his part, James cooed at her as he instructed, encouraged, and rewarded.

"That's it little one, enjoy yourself. But, don't forget your place or your priorities. I shan't be pleased if you neglect the underside."

Heeding his constructive counsel, Missy mouthed and tongued each teste. She used her nose to lift one in order to better access the underside of the other. Her tongue was wet and wanting as it stretched to delve into crevices never before navigated. Moaning, she tasted of the forbidden fruit and wanted for more.

Whore!

Unawares, her hips ground against the richly-upholstered sofa. With animalistic abandon, her engorged clit pursued its own relief. Thus far without success. That sad circumstance changed when James was kind enough to slide one leg between her sopping thighs. At long last, her brazen pussy found purchase. Shameless, Missy bucked at his shin. Her primal scream was muffled against his scrotum as her mind and body exploded in orgasm.

James held her immobile. It was some time before the tremors and twitching even began to subside. Her still spasming pussy soaked through the material of his pant leg. Her wheezing breath warmed his balls as she did her best to swallow the entire sac with her greedy mouth. Sadly, the panting orifice could accommodate only one heavy, succulent ball at a time. The other was relegated to rest stickily against her chin.

It would not to be forsaken.

Whore!

Chapter 31

Christ, I'm only human!

James was fast approaching the point of no return. The urgency he was experiencing left him with a difficult, and immediate, choice. At that moment, it was difficult to imagine he'd gone nearly three years without sex. Without *wanting* sex!

With Herculean self-discipline, he groaned as he pulled Missy's face from the depths beneath his balls. She slid weakly down his leg and into a crumpled heap on the cold, tiled floor. Allowing her little time to recover, James repositioned himself on the edge on the sofa. With the aid of her disheveled hair, he drew her swollen lips to the head of his now-impatient cock.

He relished the alarm that crosses her face, even as her lips parted to accommodate. She mistakenly assumed that a nice, tidy, vanilla blow job was expected. James smiled inwardly as he watched her squeeze her eyes shut in distaste. The thick veins in his cock thrummed with an overload of hot blood.

"Open your eyes, little one. I have a surprise for you."

Self-consciously, Missy opened her dazed eyes to gaze unveiled into his. He swore he could see to the very core of her submissive soul. Smiling with pride, he proceeded to wipe oozing pre-cum into her nostrils and across her lips. James told her how absolutely stunning she looked, and he meant every word.

With strong fingers gently gripping her jaw, he drew her dumbfounded countenance up to his and kissed her deeply. Passionately.

Perfectly.

Peeling his lips from hers, James requested that she return to the change room to slip into the white corset. Displaying the patience of Job, he reiterated the simple request. That did the trick. Missy returned sufficiently to her senses to obey. Judging from the heave of her chest, he predicted that the corset was going to prove a challenge of orgasmic proportion.

Chuckling at his clever word play, he addressed Missy's retreating back.

"I'll be there presently to tie you in, pet."

James stood to stretch his long legs. He took the opportunity to explore his options and the possible ripple effect of each. The decision he'd left her with the other night was clearly decided in his favor. Or rather, *their* favor.

True, actual words weren't spoken. Yet, her reply was evidenced by her humping and grinding on his leg like a shameless bitch in heat. Not to mention her face being contentedly buried somewhere between his ball sac and his asshole.

His stiff cock jerked at the pleasant memories. It jutted free and undeterred from the zipper of his once perfectly pressed trousers. Now, they were stained with the viscous evidence of Missy's desire. Slimy threads of pre-cum leaked from his raging dick, adding his DNA to the gooey mess.

James made up his mind as to the necessary course of action. With the issue now resolved, seven confident strides carried him to the changing room door. He flung it open without courtesy of knocking. In his world, courtesy meant something else entirely.

Missy was a sight for sore, Dominant eyes. Upon his

unheralded arrival, she twirled around barefooted in the confined space, her lips a perfect O of surprise. She'd just pulled the lace corset up over the sexy ruffles of the sheer panties. Now, she was clutching it against her bosom with both hands.

Unbeknownst to her, this instinctive response only served to force the luscious mounds upwards and outwards towards him – even without the corset being bound. Leaning against the narrow door frame, James accepted the nonverbal invitation. Reaching out, he scooped one quivering beauty from the confines of the bodice. After several moments of leering approval, he freed the second.

Burying his face in the proffered cleavage, James inhaled her scent as he tongued each globe. Her lovely titties trembled and quaked as her breath hissed from between swollen lips. The accompanying yelps and squeals caused his dick to lurch. Through it all, Missy remained in place. In fact, she went so far as to squeeze her shoulder blades together, affording James easier access.

"Such a good whore!"

He commended her for the posture correction, noting that she all but swooned from the few words of praise.

"Now, eyes down, little one."

Leaning back, he observed her bulbous, bullet-hard nipples. The left was still more turgid than the right, the fetching result of his devoted attention the previous evening. He also noticed a charming selection of tiny bruises which encircled and encompassed both areola. James grinned, reaching out with both hands. Ever-so-softly, he caressed the distended nipples. The result was a melodious selection of unbidden moans and sighs.

"Where is the chain I gifted you with, girl? Why is it not around your neck where it belongs?"

She startled at his sudden change in tone and topic. He was impressed when she was able to respond, considering the awkwardness of her position and the fact that he continued to maul both throbbing nubbins.

"Sir, I desperately wanted to wear it, but couldn't. It goes against store policy."

The acceptable explanation quickly devolved into unintelligible moans of confused desire.

"Squat down, whore, knees spread wide. I wish to enjoy the sight of your cunt leaking into those expensive panties. Clasp your hands behind your head, as well. We wouldn't want them getting in the way."

Somehow, Missy maneuvered herself into the requisite position. Properly situated at last, there was very little wiggle room. James knew that from Missy's vantage point, there was but one object within her field of vision.

That object was his raging, dripping cock...

Chapter 32

A week ago, Missy couldn't have dreamed that today she'd be squatting in a change room with her legs spread whorishly wide and her hands clasped obediently behind her head.

Further, had anyone dared to insinuate the possibility, she'd have known them to be stark raving mad. Disregarding their assertion as sheer lunacy, she'd be sure to make a wide, cautious circle around the crazy individual. Suggestions of such unrefined carnality went far beyond the acceptable bounds of respectability.

Acceptable to whom, exactly?

The rebellious query popped into her head from seemingly nowhere, taking Missy by surprise. A lifetime of societal indoctrination was suddenly little more than a fat load of hooey. Far more pressing was her immediate conundrum. It revolved around her inability to lean forward without losing her balance. A mere inch or two was all that was required. Just enough to inhale his scent and nuzzle at the head of his oozing cock.

Whore!

"Go ahead and suck, my lovely. You've earned it. I can feel how badly you want it."

She literally reeled at the words. James' 20/20 insight into her most shameful desires floored her. Without thinking, she removed her hands from behind her head in a misguided attempt to steady her emotions. Immediately, she knew it to be a mistake.

"I am in no mood for more of your insolence, girl! Get those hands back behind your head!"

And with that, he pushed her back against the dressing room wall. It was such close quarters that she remained squatting. In short order his sticky cock nudged, impatient at her lips. They stretch obscenely wide in order to accommodate the impolite breach.

Pinned to the wall by his throbbing hard-on, Missy was powerless to do anything other than gurgle. Unable to swallow, his ever-thickening cock explored the limits of her gag reflex. Slimy threads of saliva escaped her lips to dribble unchecked onto the elegant corset, mortifying her further.

While she'd given the odd blow job in her life, she was far from experienced. Nonetheless, Missy understood this was not your garden variety fellatio. She was *giving* nothing. James was taking as he saw fit. The whole while, her pussy dispensed its need as though the ruffled panties didn't exist.

Whore!

"Take it all, there's a good girl."

She heard his deep, irresistible voice cooing encouragement as though she had some choice in the matter. He urged her on, ramming his cock further down her throat than she imagined possible.

"Mind those teeth, girl. Show some respect!"

With her head all but bouncing off the wall, she focused solely on the task at hand. She endured the awkward position long past the time when her thigh and calf muscles began to complain. Her hands remained clasped behind her head, relying on his cock for stability. Not one iota of consideration was given to the snot and mascara running down her face. Missy began to wonder if and when she might be allowed to draw breath.

His next words inflamed her imagination, as well as her

nipples. Amazed, she actually felt them thicken and lengthen, as if begging for attention. *His* attention.

"Master has a reward for you, little one. Be sure to prove yourself worthy of such and swallow every drop."

There was no further warning. His cock became a steel piston in her over-stuffed mouth. James grunted through the entirety of his powerful release. The first gush of hot semen deposited itself directly into her belly, no swallowing required. She thought she would pass out from lack of oxygen when, finally, he pulled back. James growled for her to stick out her tongue. Once extended, James blew stream after stream of a massive load into her mouth and over her tongue.

By default, large globules landed on her chin and chest. *I've failed him!* She paid not a moment's consideration to her cum-splattered appearance.

She did, however, feel the failure as keenly as she would physical pain...

Chapter 33

James, on the other hand, could not have been more delighted.

He squeezed the last droplets of cum from the head of his cock, wiping them across the bridge of Missy's nose. Kneeling down to her level, he smiled into her mess of a face. His seed was congealing in the cool air, dripping from her chin to her chest. Her mouth was full of it, her tongue coated.

To James, she was breathtaking. Magnificent. With two fingers, he wiped the mucusy mess from her lips and inserted it into her already cum-filled mouth. Allowing her to swallow, he repeated the process as required. James massaged the last traces into her tongue and gums. He smiled when her little tongue poked out to lick her bruised lips.

Gathering her shivering body into his arms, he nuzzled his lips into her hair. He felt her breathing slow as her nervous system calmed. While this girl was quickly making her way into his heart, he was quite sure she'd always existed in his soul.

"Don't forget your manners, little one. What do you say when your Master rewards you so generously?"

James awaited the requisite 'Thank you, sir'.

"I love you, Master."

Taken completely off guard, James rose to an upright position in the cramped closet, Missy in his arms. He kissed her eager, cum-coated mouth. It took a moment for his words to find their way around the lump in his throat.

"Your words please me greatly, little one. You are where you are meant to be, whether in my arms or at my feet."

James watched her exhale contentedly through bloated

lips. He then pushed open the doors to the main salon to find the cooperative Teresa waiting to escort them from the deserted boutique. Unashamedly, Missy laid one cum-sticky cheek against the lapel of his suit jacket and melted into him.

"Master loves his precious whore, as well."

James mouthed the words against her ear. As he carried her through the two story glass doors and out into the night, his vision suddenly blurred.

Chapter 34

The sensation of wholeness that permeated her in this man's presence was too blissfully pure to disregard. Missy realized that James was her drug, and she was desperately addicted. She would do whatever was necessary to get her next fix.

They sat in a candle lit corner of Dominic's Crab Cave. If it were any brighter, the sprinkling of dried semen that clung to her thickened lips would be much more apparent. Missy's legs were splayed whorishly wide beneath the table of the jam packed eatery. Her breathing was more akin to panting. It stunk of cum.

She was particularly grateful for the cheery checkered tablecloth that spilled well past the table's edge. It stood as the sole barrier between maintaining what little dignity remained her and public disgrace.

Missy couldn't swear as to the details of their arrival. How they'd negotiated the short trip between the boutique and this opulent restaurant was a blur. She did, however, recall the maitre'd fawning over James upon their arrival. In no time, they were seated at one of the most coveted tables in the house. Scented candles were lit. Linen napkins materialized in their laps. The hostess sashayed away with a smile so bright, it verged on the ridiculous.

Now, James' index and middle finger were sloshing about in Missy's still-sopping pussy. It was necessary for him to reach across her thigh in order to effectively perform the lewd task. James Colton was nothing if not effective. Missy's pulse trip hammered at the base of her throat. Still, she sat compliant.

Submissive...

Master loves his precious whore as well. The extraordinary words had reverberated in her head since he'd whispered them into her ear. There could be no discounting the pervasive calm she'd felt in his arms. It persisted as he'd carried her past her groveling boss and out the extravagant doors of the boutique.

It persisted still...

Chapter 35

"Your cock sucking skills leave much to be desired, my dear. You'll either learn to suck like a decent whore, or I can simply face-fuck you as became necessary this afternoon. Your choice, of course."

The offhanded and grossly indecent rebuke jolted Missy back to the here and now. She gasped when her traitorous pussy clenched in response, embracing his buried fingers. Her excitement was appallingly evident. It was gushing over his knuckles.

Whore!

Arriving at the table, the tuxedoed waiter's eyes widened. They tracked James' extended arm to where it vanished none-too-subtly beneath the table. Even with the commotion of the boisterous dinner throng, there could be no mistaking the sloshing sounds that James' fingers elicited from deep within her.

It took about three seconds for the young waiter to piece it together. Once he connected the dots, he lit up like he'd been plugged into an electrical outlet. A leering grin spread across his face. In tandem, scorching disgrace spread across Missy's.

Without missing a stroke, James ordered garden salads, garlic toast, and six ounce lobster tails for each of them. Attentive as he and the waiter discussed the details of a dirty gin martini, Missy suddenly became aware of her ravenous hunger. For the first time in a long while, her mouth was watering for something other than James.

When their meal arrived, he made quite the production of extracting his two gooey digits from between her thighs.

He held them in front of her face, having her raise her downcast eyes in order to fully appreciate the situation. His teasing words spoke to his confidence in her impending obedience.

"Don't you think you should clean your mess, my dear?"

Missy was positive her throbbing head was about to explode. At the same time, the waiter's eyes bulged in anticipation of what was sure to be the thrill of his young life. Mesmerized by the events playing out before him, he ignored the rising crescendo of impatient diners clamoring for service.

As if instinctual, Missy's puffy, tingling lips parted. Just when they did, James repositioned his hand. Now, it was just out of reach, forcing her to lean forward in active participation. Managing to maintain the perfect posture, Missy engulfed the slimy extremities. *Up to the third and final glistening knuckle, no less!*

Focusing solely on the glowing pride and absolute acceptance shining from his eyes, she gluttonously suckled both fingers. With reverence, she moved on to pay each the individual attention it merited. She concluded by lapping betwixt the two, so as not to miss a drop.

"Good girl!"

Missy swooned. James' simple endorsement filled her with prideful self-satisfaction. Sitting up, she just caught the waiter's retreating back. At long last, he was scurrying off to attend the swelling ranks of disgruntled and famished diners. Amazed by her newly minted lack of modesty, she giggled at the incredible tale the boy would soon be sharing. Vaguely, she wondered if anyone would believe him.

In any case, Missy had no doubt that the young man

would remember the spectacle he'd just witnessed for the rest of his days.

As would she...

Chapter 36

Missy hunched miserably on the toilet. She felt weak and queasy after a restless night spent alternating between hot and cold sweats. Blurry-eyed, she squinted at the elevated reading on the thermometer.

Swallowing with difficulty, she pondered whether her aching throat was yet another symptom of the sudden illness. She concluded that, more likely, it was a natural by-product of having James' cock jammed down it—repeatedly!

She might have hung her head in morning-after indignation, were she not overcome with the urgent need to vomit. Scrambling off the toilet, she was thankful to make it to her knees before the retching and heaving turned into violent waves of projectile puking. What little remained of the previous evening's mouthwatering meal now floated in the toilet.

And mouthwatering it was. Almost as yummy as the company. They'd spent the balance of the evening eating and talking and laughing. The service was, not surprisingly, spectacular. Their vaguest whim was the attentive waiter's immediate priority.

After the scrumptious meal, James ordered a cognac for himself, and for Missy a bowl of ice cream smothered in chocolate sauce. She'd coveted it earlier as it floated past their table atop a server's tray. When it arrived, James instructed her to sit up straight, and to fold her hands in her lap.

He proceeded to spoon feed ice cream into her mouth as one might a child. He was quite adept at scooping it up with a flourish of the spoon when it 'accidentally' dribbled down her chin. This morning, that very same chocolate sauce was floating in the toilet bowl along with other, less recognizable delicacies. Missy vowed never to eat again.

James had wanted, no, *needed*, to know everything about her. Beginning with birth, it seemed. They snuggled close as she unreservedly divulged all. No topic was taboo. He was an attentive listener, appearing not at all surprised by introspective recollections of her teenaged years.

Over time, the frightening suspicion that she was different from the other girls turned to abject certainty. That fearsome surety affected her life in a multitude of ways, none of them affirmative.

Submissive...

While James hung enraptured on her every syllable, he offered precious little in return. When she came close to passing out mid-sentence into the dregs of her ice cream, he delivered her safely home. Accompanying her to the door, he bid her goodnight with a chaste kiss to the forehead. Before she could utter a sound, he'd turned, navigated the porch's rickety stairs—and disappeared into the darkness.

Now, she sat crumpled on the bathroom floor, flushed cheek resting against cold porcelain. Work was out of the question. Evidently, the wooziness and chills which plagued her the previous evening were of dual origin. They weren't exclusive to the lewd and lascivious acts that played havoc with her nervous system. Acts, she reminded herself, in which she'd been only too eager to participate.

Her eyes slid to the chic, monogrammed bag resting against the foot of her bed. Was it the fever, or was it really glaring back at her accusingly? The designer bag was from Ebony&Ivory. Inside were the pricey negligee and corset she'd 'modeled' for James.

What little equilibrium remained her evaporated at the thought of the sexy, once-virginal frillies. Hugging the toilet bowl closer, she deemed it the perfect opportunity to assess her unladylike conduct of the previous evening. After all, she was already nauseous.

"Maybe being sick has an unexpected silver lining."

Missy croaked the words in the direction of her own vomit. Her face flushed with prickly heat, having nothing to do with the budding malaise. It was more to do with her not being able to look her boss or Stephanie in the eye.

Was that really me grinding on his leg like some desperate bitch in heat? The simple undertaking of shaking her head in disbelief only nauseated her further. It appeared that the penance for her animalistic behavior the night before was feeling like dog shit this morning!

Groaning with effort, Missy flushed the toilet and rose slowly to brush her teeth. Lightheaded, she squinted at the clock. It was still too early to call in sick. Clutching her cell phone, she crawled between clammy sheets. It was only by chance that she noticed the text message.

She marveled at how seeing a solitary message from James caused her heart to lurch. This fascinating man captivated her utterly, igniting feelings and desires never before imagined. With a glance or a word, he garnered her complete attention.

She read the missive, savoring each syllable as though the tenderest of morsels: *Good morning, cherished whore. I trust you slept well. Have a wonderful day thinking of me. Do not forget to wear the chain.*

Of its own accord, her hand fluttered to her throat, around which the exquisite silver filament was fastened.

Astounding really, how quickly and readily she'd morphed. Missy was transformed from the skittish, self-reliant woman she'd always been, to a James-needy, yet oddly serene, submissive 'whore'.

She couldn't respond fast enough. Her clammy fingers flew. She typed that she was running a temperature and sick to her stomach. That there was no way she could manage work. She added that she was back in bed, and finished by wishing him a wonderful day. Once done, she fell asleep instantly, phone still in hand.

Missy slept heavily. Right up until the doorbell chimed...

Chapter 37

James stood on the front steps of the tiny bungalow, heart melting. He surveyed the dilapidation that darkness had obscured the night before. Missy's attempts to distract the eye from the escalating disrepair were both creative and charming. They were also hopeless.

The rotting floorboards of the porch were painted a welcoming blue. Long ago, they had conceded to the supremacy of the elements. Now, they lay faded and warped in defeat. Rusted door hinges refused to be camouflaged beneath thick coats of identical blue. Duct tape fashioned into the shape of daisies covered most of the holes in the screen door. Vases of plastic wildflowers surrounded an over-sized wicker armchair that was conspicuously out of proportion on the tiny veranda.

James eyed the flimsy lock on the even flimsier front door, skeptical of its veracity. It joggled when manipulated from within in response to his unexpected arrival. *This will never do!* He made a mental note to contact his handyman and a locksmith.

The weather-beaten door swung open and there stood a none-too-thrilled Christopher. The previous evening, Missy spoke at length about her only child. Her edges softened, her eyes shimmered, and her voice filled with love and pride whenever his name was mentioned.

Nearly seventeen years old, he was a fine looking young man. James guessed his height at about five foot eight or nine. His facial features were his own, but his build was reminiscent of his mother's. Lean and compact, he stood in the opened doorway wearing nothing but a pair of cotton boxers. Red-rimmed eyes squinted against the dual assault of doorbells and sunlight. James spoke first.

"You must be Christopher. I'm James, James Colton. Your mom might have mentioned me?"

He extended his hand and waited for Christopher to shake it. Likely unaccustomed to greetings more formal than, "Hey man, wazz'up?", it took a moment or two for the gesture to register. At last, Christopher reached out to perform his part in the unfamiliar ritual.

When he did grasp James' outstretched limb, his fervor was surprising. He pumped it vigorously, switching to a two-handed grip. A mischievous grin spread across his young face as he invited James in. Not waiting for a reply, he practically yanked him through the opened doorway.

"Yeah, she might have mentioned your name. Maybe even told me a little about you. But mostly, it's her gawd awful singing and goofy grin that tells me what I need to know."

Relinquishing the stranglehold on James' extremity, Christopher lowered his voice.

"She never used to do a whole lot of either."

James felt his heart soften, expanding to make room for this caring boy. His mother's voice had quavered when she'd spoken of Christopher's deadbeat father. In hushed tones, she'd imparted how Luke drank a staggering amount of champagne at their wedding. The momentous occasion ended with her in tears, and him unconscious and drooling on the head table.

Thereafter, Luke's only marriage was to the bottle. Thanks to his unswerving devotion, his volume and consumption escalated at an impressive rate. He strove for, and attained, the proficiency level of expert. In any other vocation, he would have stood as a glorious example of what was possible when one dedicated themselves to fulfilling their objectives.

As often happens in life, one talent can lead to another. This principle proved true in Luke's case. In record breaking time, he was able to add *'incapable of maintaining employment'* to his short but infamous resume. It wasn't long before he was faced with the dilemma of choosing between booze and supporting his family.

He'd bought a half-gallon of vodka to help him with that momentous decision. Shortly thereafter, Luke was suckling at the government's teat for even the most basic of sustenance.

The exact opposite of a strong paternal role model. James was disgusted. Boys need a real man's influence if they're to grow up with the proper appreciation of a real man's responsibilities. The protective son interrupted his thoughts.

"I gotta tell you, though, dude, if ya hurt her, I'm gonna have to kill ya!"

Christopher's attempt at manly bravado trailed off in self-conscious giggles. Still, James very much wanted to reassure him of his intentions. Never once did he break eye contact with the boy.

"Neither you nor your mother have anything to fear from me, son. I would be proud to care for you both, if you'd allow me that honor. A real man takes his responsibilities very seriously, Christopher."

Chapter 38

Christopher returned the eye-contact unwaveringly, scouring James' face for any sign of deception. After an extended silence that should have turned awkward but didn't, he spoke three words.

"I believe you."

His mom operated under the misconception that she protected him from the brutal waste of skin that was his father. She wanted to believe that he never witnessed the son-of-a-bitch grabbing and shoving her. That somehow, he missed the dark circles under her eyes and the anxiety that too often etched itself into her features.

Truth was, he'd never heard her say a nasty word about the very nasty man. Still, Christopher wasn't blind. He was aware that all too often, she'd hand over her hard earned money to the bully. After all, the man needed to drink. It was a far higher priority than than his progeny's needing to eat!

It pissed him off, no question. His mom deserved so much more. She deserved a man who would treat her right. One who would protect her where he was unable. Very soon, he was leaving for college. With all these things in mind, Christopher measured the sincerity in James' eyes against the unaccustomed lilt in his mother's voice.

He decided that James Colton deserved the benefit of the doubt. There wasn't a wink of treachery in his eyes. Just the opposite, in fact. With that out of the way, Christopher was ready to move on to the next item on the agenda: the business of why James, or anybody else for that matter, would drop in at this unholiest of hours!

He wasn't aware of the mother's unheralded illness.

He'd stayed up all night to study for finals—and to play video games. He helped James locate the fixings for hot honeyed tea, chattering on about his upcoming graduation. Christopher worried about his future. He also worried about his mom, no matter how often she insisted he not.

"It's not like mom volunteering to work overtime every day makes that much of a difference, ya know? I keep telling her it's not worth it to kill herself, and she keeps asking me who the parent is around here."

Christopher shrugged, smiling into James' concerned eyes.

"Ya can't fight city hall, ya know!"

Accompanying James along the short hallway, he paused at the first door.

"Nice to meet you, Mr. Colton."

He surprised himself with his unaccustomed deference. He watched as James transferred the steaming mug to his left hand, extending his right. It was clear that he meant to repeat the revered hand pumping ritual. Now, it was James who was smiling.

"Listen, son, I can't stay long. I have to get to work. Is it too much to ask that you 'study' for another hour or so? I'd like to ask a small favor of you before I leave."

Christopher grinned at his emphasis on the word 'study'. This time, he was confident in his handshake. Closing his door behind him, he heard Mr. Colton making his way down the hall towards his mother's bedroom...

Chapter 39

"You shan't need that, my dear."

Without benefit of knocking, James entered the sanctuary of Missy's bedroom as if it were his own. He assumed she'd heard the early morning commotion. She was out of bed, attempting to wrap a housecoat around her otherwise naked body.

Not having heard him enter the room, Missy froze, gaping with shock. She looked as though she was seeing a ghost, or hallucinating from fever.

"Good morning, little one."

With three short strides he was at her side, transferring the warm mug into her ice cold hands. Solicitously, he helped her out of the robe she'd pulled closer about her. James was well aware that it was the first time she'd stood nude before him.

He could intuit her frantic thoughts as though they were his own. Her internal angst was compounded by the fact that she was sick to her stomach and looked like crap. He hadn't exactly caught her at her finest hour. She was definitely *not* ready for her close-up, Mr. DeMille!

James determined this to be a significant moment in her submission to him. And likewise, in his Dominance of her. Hanging the robe on the chair that served double duty as night stand, he made himself comfortable on the edge of her single bed. He gathered her clammy, shivering body into his arms, pulling her gently to stand between his legs.

Because he could, he pressed his face between her bobbling, goose-fleshed tits and inhaled. Positioned conveniently before him, why would he not? He spoke, not bothering to disengage from the multitude of delights to be realized between a woman's breasts.

"Understand, little one, that to me, you are beautiful. This illness has no bearing on how I see you today, just as age will have no bearing on how I see you in the future. Mainstream ideals of beauty have no place in my reality."

Drawing her onto his lap, James set the tea on the bedside table/chair. Holding her chin with one hand, he looked into her pale, perspiring, make-up-free face.

"Or, should I say—*our* reality. It was the strength of your warrior heart and the perfection of your submissive soul which first captivated me. Only later did I become aware of your exquisite physical beauty. Hear me well girl, that you may always feel beautiful in my presence."

He asked if she understood but no words were forthcoming. Missy sniffled, blew her nose mightily, and swallowed hard, as though trying to dislodge a balloon from her throat. When at last capable of speech, her husky words pleased him very much.

"I understand perfectly, sir. I am beautiful..."

Chapter 40

Where did the time go?

Catching a glimpse of the timepiece flashing at his wrist, Missy was jolted into frantic action. Even nauseous, she was overcome with an unheralded peacefulness in this man's lap. It was not her desire to vacate it. Nonetheless, after yesterday's fiasco, she couldn't afford any missteps where Teresa was concerned. She wriggled from James' lap.

Or...tried to.

He stopped her cold. Gathering both of her wrists into one of his large hands, he applied just enough pressure to render her motionless. Her naked breasts were now squashed obscenely together. James was blatant as he ogled them. Missy's bloodshot eyes shot open, followed by her mouth.

"Sir, I have to call Teresa and let her know I won't be in. I can't be late. Again."

His wordless response was to apply more pressure to her already confined wrists. There was no need to 'tell' her a third time. She stopped her fretting. When he spoke, it was in the most courteous and gentlemanly of fashions.

"Would you allow me to look after that little conundrum on your behalf, pet?"

The pressure at her wrists was steady, unrelenting. Without question, she was his prisoner, bound at both wrists and heart. Even so, this immobilizing truth played no part in her prompt response. Exhaling a lifetime's worth of tension, all she could manage was to nod in grateful assent.

Missy surrendered herself to the irresistible force of nature that was James...

Chapter 41

Women must literally fall at his feet! I certainly did.

Giggling at the double entendre, Missy wasn't at all surprised when he pulled out his phone and located Teresa's private number in his directory. Once again, she speculated as to when in the past he'd frequented the boutique. And, for whom?

She never considered herself the jealous type, but in fairness, she'd never been tested. Now, she felt the razor-sharp talons of green envy clawing at her consciousness. Even allowing for the befuddling haze of nausea and fever, she was dismayed to discover herself capable of such intense and unwarranted feelings.

Of course this extraordinary man has a past. Truth be told, she wouldn't want it any other way. How could she allow herself to follow if he weren't capable of leading with the wisdom borne only from experience?

With these thoughts in mind, Missy massaged her just-released wrists. Her eyes slid once again to the bag containing the two stunning pieces of lingerie. Flashing back, she relived the carnal events of the previous day. Teresa had all but shoved them into the private dressing room. Locking the door behind them, she'd broken every rule in her own book – *and* thrown away the key!

Now, the sordid secrets of that afternoon lurked within the depths of that sophisticated carrier. Both dainty garments had accompanied them into that dressing room. Both were now stained with the sticky, undeniable evidence of her enthusiastic participation. One was also heavily spattered with James' semen.

Her face burned equally from fever and shame. Missy considered whether the minor illness was also a blessing in disguise. After all, she did not mind postponing face time with Teresa. Not one little bit.

James' smooth, commanding voice interrupted her musings as easily as a knife through hot butter. Engrossed by both pitch and tempo, she hung on his every syllable. As expected, he notified Teresa that she was ill and unable to make it to work. It was the next sentence out of his mouth that sent Missy tumbling to the floor in shock and disbelief.

Was she hallucinating, or did he just give Teresa her two-week notice?

"Tsk, tsk, girl. I avert my attention for a single moment only to find you mucking about on the floor? And, not even in the proper kneeling position?"

Her eyes were two harvest moons in the pale dusk of her face. Her gaping mouth produced a third. Running a warm finger around her parched lips, James smiled, unperturbed.

"We shall have to work on that, shan't we, pet?"

As a concession to her not feeling well, James declined to chastise her for the absence of an immediate, and of course, affirmative response. Instead, he helped her as she clumsily rose to her feet. He then snuggled her naked body back onto his lap. He was well aware that she perceived her world as having just been turned inside out and upside down.

In fact, just the opposite was true. When fat, shimmy tears threatened, James turned her ever-so-gently towards him. Lifting her chin, he held her gaze with his. The earnestness he wished to convey came straight from his heart.

"Little one, I promised to provide for you and your son. I ask that you have faith in my doing precisely that. You will find it is not in my nature to make rash decisions. Nor do I shirk my responsibilities."

"This was not done for the purpose of binding the submissive to the Master. Trust me, there are far more amusing and less costly methods of accomplishing that."

A grin played on his lips and he didn't bother to suppress it. He let it have its way, but didn't continue until all traces of it were gone.

"This was done, my love, so that you can understand that the Master is irrevocably bound to the submissive. I can at any time ascertain employment on your behalf, and at a much higher standard than that which you just vacated. I give you my word as a Dominant and a gentleman, should you ever become discontent with the life I provide. Do you trust me, little one?"

Her eyes glowed, but this time, not from tears. The expression that spread across her countenance was nothing short of dazzling. Kissing each corner of her dry, fevered lips, James spoke directly into her opened mouth.

"In truth my love, what I did *was* terribly selfish. What I have in mind for you will make it seem but a pittance!"

Chapter 42

Missy's belly was centered perfectly between his spread thighs, her jiggling ass a vision worthy of launching ships. Without warning, James had flipped her onto her stomach, then paused to take in the luscious view.

He no longer wondered why he found the female bottom so much more alluring when crisscrossed with the stripes left by a well-slotted spatula. It was simply the way it was, as far back as he could remember. While it saddened him to see the delightful marks fading, he was quite sure she would merit further chastisement in the not too distant future.

James was a patient man. He could wait.

There was no doubt that Missy could feel his stiffening cock as it burgeoned against her hip. He stroked and squeezed what was his to behold.

"Now then, let's see how that fever is doing and get you back into bed, shall we? Be still now, girl. I don't have all day."

So tickled was James with his next thought that he shared the witticism with Missy.

"After all, my precious—some of us have to work for a living!"

Humming tunelessly, James reached into his jacket pocket and withdrew two items. He took care to position them within Missy's line of vision. When her entire body stiffened against his thighs, he knew the placement was perfect. A groan of comprehension escaped her lips. She very nearly levitated off his lap.

Without preamble, James thrust two unyielding digits into an already swollen cunt. He chortled with amusement as the irrefutable confirmation of her excitement leaked onto his fingers.

"You like what you see, don't you whore?"

Although still grinning, this time he expected an answer and was out of patience with her dawdling.

"Don't you whore?"

An accompanying smack to each glorious ass cheek elicited the positive response he sought, and in very short order, too. As an added bonus, a pair of scarlet palm prints emerged, one per buttock. The delectable sight caused his cock to jerk, demanding attention. Pre-cum oozed within the tight confines of his pants.

I go three years without any sex at all, and now, I can't make it three days? It was going to be his pleasure to take out his newly-awakened sexual frustrations on, and *in,* the exquisite ass that was writhing in his lap.

Based on her reaction, he presumed Missy had never seen an anal thermometer or a butt plug before. She gawked speechless at both. Even if she were able to form comprehensive sentences, she was in no position for discourse.

"Now, I need some assistance in order to properly care for you, pet."

He spoke nonchalantly, knowing full well that his next words would send her world spiraling off its axis for the second time that morning.

"Please arch your back, reach around, and spread open that sweet ass of yours..."

Chapter 43

James helped her waddle to his office. She leaned heavily on his arm for support. Once inside, he immediately requested that she assume the proper kneeling position.

"You must be very impatient for me to use your ass by now, pet."

James persisted, relishing the stunned horror on Missy's beautiful face.

"Happily, we are in total accordance on that subject!"

He was well aware of the fat, stainless steel butt plug that governed her every move. After all, he'd installed it. It was held in place thanks to the strength and stamina of her clenched ass-cheeks. That and sheer determination.

The hefty encumbrance turned his simple request to kneel into a thorny calculation on her part. A calculation that proved highly entertaining to observe as she attempted to solve it. Her brow furrowed as she concentrated on its resolution.

Submissive...

When she was at last suitably situated, he rewarded her with a cursory 'Good girl'. Her eyes all but gleamed from the two simple words of approval. With her head pressed adoringly against his thigh, James absently stroked her hair.

"The day will come when you beg for me in your ass, little one. You will have a deep ache to be stretched by your Master's hardness."

Of its own volition, his mind rewound to a time long past, and a wife long dead. Angeline. Her strict religious upbringing taught her that anal sex was immoral, improper, and just plain dirty. Deeply indoctrinated, she maintained a healthy fear of the fire and brimstone hell that awaited those lost souls who dared to indulge.

Years after her memorable 'initiation', he'd been surprised to learn that she'd prayed long and hard for the salvation of his deviant soul. Often, he'd teased her about it. But, not nearly as often as she'd begged him to take her anally!

James smiled at the bittersweet memory, even as he murmured to Missy.

"It is the ultimate offering of a submissive to her Master, little one. I can almost taste how badly you desire it."

James was rewarded with the immediate and sharp intake of her breath. He was quite confident that, for Missy, the room was spinning as though she'd had more than a few too many. Sober and fully recouped from the flu, there would be no doubt as to the source of her vertigo.

They hadn't seen each other since that memorable morning two days previous when he brought her a cup of tea to assuage her illness. He'd also impolitely introduced her to the fat rectal thermometer and the even fatter butt plug that she sported today. She'd been so kind to assist him by spreading her own ass-cheeks.

The chubby butt plug was the perfect accessory to the ultra-short skirt, sky-high heels, and sheer blouse she was wearing today. As expected, she was braless. He'd assessed the new ensemble with a connoisseur's eye the moment she'd emerged from her car. Without a doubt, it was well worth the investment.

Standing before her in his office, he made quite a production of stripping down. It would be her first time seeing him completely nude. Watching her eyes widen in appreciation and apprehension was highly satisfying. Not to mention arousing.

His engorged cock jutted from his tanned, well-muscled body. In no mood to put up with much more dilly-dallying, it jerked and oozed in exasperation. Noticing the sticky head was conveniently located just inches from Missy's mouth, he decided to avail himself.

He gathered silky, auburn tresses into a manageable handful on the top of her head, tightened his grip imperceptibly, and gave his whore permission to suck...

Chapter 44

Missy heard his unnerving words as though through a megaphone and a vacuum at the same time. He'd made sure she was well aware of her impending future.

Now, he was enjoying her discomfiture as she processed the overload of information. When she leaned forward to take his manhood into her mouth, he pulled away. She was forced to use her upper lip to reach the final few centimeters that his hand entangled in her hair disallowed.

The two days they'd spent apart seemed an eternity to Missy. She was only allowed to remove the butt plug when using the toilet or bathing. And even then, only if necessary. It served as a constant reminder of James, leaving her weak and wanting.

It served another, unexpected purpose, as well. The Lucite plug was a constant reminder of the fantasies that had tormented her since adolescence. The shame and guilt she'd experienced as a result of these 'revolting' desires was indescribable. When they became a recurrent theme that she couldn't, or *wouldn't,* defend against—the humiliation intensified tenfold.

Yet, here she was happily slurping on this man's cock. The size of him was nothing less than terrifying in relation to the size of her. Stretching her lips wide, she labored to accommodate.

James urged her on, encouraging her to greater lengths. Excuse the pun. He took pains to clarify that the harder the cock, the better to fuck her up the ass. Mortified, she became aware of thick pussy juice making its way down her inner thighs.

Whore!

Sighing, Missy knew his assessment of her to be one hundred percent accurate. She was, and had always been, a submissive whore bereft of her soul mate. Soul *Master*. It was stunning, really, how easily he'd penetrated her reinforced facade. The closet door was all but ripped from its hinges. In an instant, her deepest, darkest secrets were exposed.

On her knees at his feet, her intent was simply to make him the happiest man in the world. This thought alone enabled her to take his cock just that much further down her distended throat.

Without notice, he withdrew, his fingers still secured in Missy's tangled locks. Taking full advantage of the leverage, he dragged her to the back of the sofa. She thought she heard growling but couldn't be sure over the deafening din in her own head. Knowing what was about to transpire, she vacillated wildly between dread—and anticipation!

With her hips level to the sofa back, James pushed her face first into the seat cushions. Missy blushed scarlet as the rounded globes of her naked ass parted before his eyes. She could only imagine his carnal delight as the faux ruby—the sparkling crown jewel of the butt-plug, was revealed for his viewing pleasure.

She was grateful when for long moments, he did nothing but stroke the plump flesh surrounding the bulky apparatus. She couldn't possibly know that he was simply feasting upon the unspoiled splendor before him in anticipation of the ecstasy to come.

Her real anguish began when he began to twist, turn, and tug on the butt plug itself. She squealed, nearly flying upright when he succeeded in working it from the loosened orifice. Missy knew what was coming. She'd never experienced anal sex, though it was the mainstay of her fantasy life. Her heart pounded in her chest and temples. Her need oozed from her pussy.

It said her more than she was able to comprehend just then.

Her squeals turned to humiliated moans as she envisioned his eyes feasting on the gaping spectacle that was her anus. James leaned over the couch and worked a large, bubble-gum pink ball-gag between her panting lips. Tenderly kissing the back of her neck, he buckled it behind her head.

From that point on, all that remained was the pain. Pain—and mind-blowing pleasure! At what point the torment turned into exquisite ecstasy, Missy could not have said.

Whore!

Chapter 45

James used her hard. The ache in his balls combined with the overwhelming desire to have this amazing creature left him disinclined to dawdle. Appraising her degree of eagerness, he was not surprised to find her whore-wet and wanting. He crudely substituted her convenient drippings and his spittle in the place of lubricant.

He edged the head of his cock past the softened first ring, paused, then inched it through the more unyielding second. Disregarding the muffled cries and grunts rising from the vicinity of the sofa cushions, James methodically worked his way in—and then *all* the way into her tight, virgin ass.

Once embedded, he gave her sphincter an opportunity to acclimate itself to the impolite intrusion. Motionless, he took the opportunity to stroke her swollen clit. The response was unmistakable as sharp yelps of discomfort turned to weak whimpers of desire.

"Easy, little one, try to relax. There's a good girl. Know that are most stunning with my cock buried in your ass!"

It was true. The intoxicating sight before him was impossible to resist, and James was not reticent. He delivered three stinging slaps to each quivering cheek, producing what he considered to be the perfect shade of scarlet. He had no doubt that Picasso himself would be impressed. Missy's asshole contracted deliciously around his phallus in tandem with each blow.

On the sixth and final smack, her entire body convulsed as she came anally. As she moaned and shuddered, the strength of her orgasm milked his cock. There was no more holding back. At that moment, wild horses couldn't have stopped him from taking what was his. Starting slowly but quickly gaining speed, James opened her using the full length and breadth of his cock.

He spent himself copiously into her bowels, her inflamed ass spasming in response. Three long years of grief and pent-up frustration were literally washed away. Howling like a wolf at the full moon, he fell forward, blanketing her entire body with his. Face to face and gasping for air, James and Missy experienced an almost religious epiphany as his seed flowed from his body and passed into hers.

After what seemed an eternity, he withdrew his still-tumescent cock from her ravaged, leaking rectum. Ever-so-gently, he gathered her unresisting body into his arms and removed the gag. Missy's entire body was trembling, her nervous system shocked by the intensity of the experience. No doubt, the significance of submitting to such an act, and the implications of her obvious response to it, shook her to the core.

Drenched in perspiration, her mouth hung slack-jawed. Tears glittered in her mesmerizing eyes as a new understanding dawned. Her face shone with snot and spit. It also gleamed with the unmistakable joy of sweet submission. She was gorgeous. Smiling, he told her what she already knew.

"You belong to me, little one.

Chapter 46

Oozing gobs of cum onto the tiled floor of the bathroom, Missy squatted, still trembling. Her knees were splayed wide. This was the position she was to assume when she washed James' genitals with a moist, warm cloth.

She, on the other hand, was not given the same consideration. James rather enjoyed the thought of her filled with his seed. Not to mention the sight of it leaking from her bruised bottom.

She was mentally, physically, and emotionally exhausted. Yet, standing out from the haze was an all-encompassing sense of... pride? *Yes, pride!* In all her years as a valued employee at the boutique, Missy had never experienced a feeling of accomplishment equal to this.

She no longer cared if 'they' thought it was wrong—whoever they were. Society's sexual parameters were nothing if not confining and hypocritical. Often, these puritanical constraints left those of an alternative nature with a propensity towards isolation. And anxiety. In the mainstream, or 'vanilla' realm, deviations from the norm were not encouraged. Nor were they well-received.

More often than not they were met with bias, if not outright violence. Missy grimaced at the notion that if they still burned women at the stake, she'd be toast. Luckily, the only thing she need concern herself with was James's approval. At the moment, he was smiling down at her with absolute acceptance. His praise was beginning to mean more than oxygen itself.

Master...

She focused on performing the task at hand to the best

of her ability. She hoped he could discern the devotion behind every mindful stroke of the cloth. Leaning relaxed against the sink, he seemed to read her mind.

"Such a good girl you are; showing the proper appreciation of my seed in your bowels. You will always be eager to welcome me there, whether standing, kneeling or lying down. Furthermore, you shall be grateful should I choose to shed my cum there."

With her hands at his cock and her eyes level with his balls, Missy responded to the provocative words with outright candor.

"I cannot find words to express my gratitude, sir. Both for you, and for any attention you feel I warrant."

She took his silence as tacit consent to continue.

"I feel privileged to offer you not only my bottom, but all that I am."

For emphasis, she leaned forward onto bruised knees to nuzzle the tip of his cock. She'd meant every word. If not for James' sixth sense, she'd never have been granted the opportunity to freely express who she truly was. There was no going back.

He was to Missy what a life jacket was to a person drowning.

Chapter 47

At long last, she was snuggled into the same bed as this rare and distinctive man. Missy discovered that her whirling mind and ravaged body were far too stimulated to succumb to sleep.

The soothing rhythm of James' breathing as he slept soundly beside her was music to her ears. She reveled in the realization that for the first time in her life, she felt complete. Entirely in the moment, her mind, body, spirit, and yes—her very soul, were in harmony. She luxuriated in the unaccustomed absence of anxiety and the nonexistence of fear.

Feeling soft and submissive, she fingered the rigid collar so recently secured about her slender throat. The key that fit the tiny silver padlock was relegated to the depths of his desk's top drawer. Intrinsically, she'd understood the significance of the gesture.

She belonged with him and to him. She was the perfect yin to his Yang, the consummate follow to his Lead, the definitive woman to his Man. She relived the collaring ceremony for the umpteenth time in an hour.

First, James transformed the sofa in his office into a comfortably appointed queen-sized bed. Next, he sat on its edge, having her kneel up from her customary position at his feet. He removed the silver chain from around her neck. Immediately, she'd felt nervous, naked without it. Not understanding, she wondered if he was displeased with her.

He then produced a flat, square box, seemingly out of thin air. Opening it, James allowed her a glimpse of its contents. A black leather collar sat atop a cloud of shredded silver tissue paper. Polished to a deep, lustrous sheen, it was lined with luxurious sheepskin. Three sturdy, silver O-rings were placed strategically. The largest was perfectly centered while the two smaller flanked it on either side.

The rings were secured to the thick collar with what appeared to be three small, perfectly-cut diamonds. Each demanded the eye of the beholder, glittering haughtily against their backdrop of blackest leather.

Placed within the circle created by the collar was the bloom from a single red rose. Before sliding it behind her ear, he gallantly attempted to untangle her sweat and sofa-matted hair. It was a wasted effort.

Missy recounted his every word, verbatim: *This collar signifies that you belong to me unequivocally, little one. Its meaning is deep and steeped in tradition. You must recognize the gravity of this moment, and base your decision on that understanding. The choice that you make here and now is absolute. If you accept it, it will represent an immutable decision on both our parts.*

You will be my love and my whore, at my whim and for my pleasure. You will be adored, appreciated, and cherished, as shall your son. While you may be allowed input, all final decisions will be my responsibility. You are already well aware that I take each and every one of those decisions extremely seriously.

Be secure in the knowledge that your best interests are paramount, even if occasionally you find the methods employed to be somewhat perplexing.

What say you, pet? Please, speak freely...

Chapter 48

Parting her lips to respond, Missy had faltered. She understood there would be no turning back once the words were spoken. Of its own volition, her mind flashed to that remarkable day when James had dropped by unexpectedly—at six o'clock in the morning!

Bearing hot, honeyed tea to alleviate her sudden malady, he'd nonetheless exerted his dominance over her as naturally as a male dog marked its territory. She, by comparison, had been dazed and confused—and not only as a result of the flu.

She confessed to herself an insatiable hunger to be dominated and adored by this man. She would never forget the panic that gripped her when he'd taken it upon himself to resign her employment. He'd done so as coolly and calmly as one might order a ham sandwich. In fact, he'd chuckled as he conveyed the gist of his conversation with her boss.

At the same time, he'd tucked her tenderly into bed.

He fluffed flat, sweat-stained pillows and pulled the comforter to her chin. Kissing her forehead as if she were a convalescing child, he'd recounted how Teresa insisted that Missy not concern herself with the 'silly' two week notification period. Missy was convinced that had Teresa bent backwards even one millimeter further to kiss his arse, she'd be in a body brace today!

Before she could respond to James with absolute conviction, the most important detail needed to be considered. Christopher. Missy may be submissive, but she was far from lacking in intelligence. She appreciated that there were many facets to an enduring relationship. Other than the implausible collision of souls and a mutual deviance, that is.

If she were to become as reliant upon James as he was contending, it was imperative that he be there for the long haul. Yes, it was heart-warming that he drove across town to tend to her when she was under the weather. But the truest indication of his long-term intentions had come after she'd fallen into a peaceful slumber.

James wrote a check for twenty-five thousand dollars and handed it to a speechless Christopher. He'd even made it payable in Christopher's name. It was to go towards college tuition and helping his mother. He promised Christopher that if he worked hard in college and was good to his mom, another check in the same amount would be forthcoming. That was it. No strings attached.

As her son always said: ya can't fight city hall!

With trust and unconcealed love radiant in her eyes, Missy was prepared to reply to James' life-altering query. She spoke from a depth within her heart that until now had remained untapped.

"I am honored to accept your collar and to call you Master. It will be worn with the utmost of pride and the greatest of pleasure. Willingly, I place my love – and my life— in your capable hands."

Her last conscious memory before falling into a dreamless sleep was the sound of the collar's deadbolt as it slid into place.

Submissive...

Chapter 49

James woke up hard, horny, and thinking of Angeline. His cock throbbed from an acute state of rigidity. It would not recede and refused to be marginalized. Evidently, Missy rekindled a deep desire within him. A desire he thought long extinguished, and buried alongside his wife.

He and Angeline were married for eight years prior to her untimely death. It was hardly surprising that he awoke with her in his head. In fact, there was rarely a day that he didn't. This time, however, there was a distinct difference.

This time, Angeline did not restrict herself to his 'big' head.

Leaning over, he inhaled the wholesome scent of the freshly-fucked and collared girl sleeping beside him. James knew himself to be the most fortunate of men. Destiny was kind enough to smile upon him not once, but twice in the same lifetime.

He ran his hand over the swell of Missy's belly and between her thighs. She moaned softly but did not awaken. He was pleased to see that even in an unconscious state, her legs opened at his touch.

His hand came away slippery with the excretion from a still-creamy pussy. Smiling inwardly, he couldn't imagine a better lubricant for the job at hand. While usually appreciative of a clever play on words, James was impatient to get down to business. At this particular moment, he was far more interested in cock-play than word-play!

Palming his inflamed manhood, he smeared Missy's juices along the full length. Halfheartedly, James began to jerk off. He struggled to focus on the enchanting sights and sounds of that very afternoon, but failed. The reaming of Missy's delectable virgin asshole was an experience of orgasmic proportion. One that ought to be cherished, relished, and relived time and time again.

And yet, both his mind and body declined to comply. Angeline's visage continued to interject itself, refusing to be supplanted. Rudely, it disrupted his singular objective. His determination was literally shriveling away! Could she somehow sense that something was amiss? Was it possible she intuited that James was about to place her where she was long overdue: in the past?

With these mystical questions hanging unanswered, the mental dialogue ended. Without further reservation, he surrendered himself to Angeline. He understood that after too many years of grief and remorse, this would be her final send-off. First thing in the morning, James would pack up over a decade's worth of mementos and place them in storage.

At long last, the time had come.

And, now, it was his turn. Lubricating his cock with repeated contributions from Missy's generous pussy, he relaxed into the pillows.

He thought back to the first year of their relationship, before they were wed. It had been perfect in every way save one. Angeline suffered from a seemingly incurable distaste for fellatio. Her enthusiasm for, and proficiency at, the fine art of cocksucking left much to be desired.

Too much to remain sustainable, in fact. In his world— the world Angeline literally dropped to her knees and begged to become a part of—the sucking of cock was considered a mandatory life skill. As was the swallowing of semen. Expertise in these 'sensitive' areas garnered far more favor and respect than any Doctorate degree. She may not work outside of the home, but she would suck cock properly—and eagerly —within it!

Enticements were proffered, dispensed in two forms: reward and punishment. Yet, nothing proved incentive enough. No discernible progress was forthcoming. She took only the head of his heavy cock into her mouth. Adding insult to injury, her scrunched-up face conveyed her true feelings – no words required.

All that was about to change.

After playing a spirited round of golf with the usual suspects, he arrived home with an unexpected guest. His Honor George T. Weatherly, respected adjudicator and beloved husband, had moaned non-stop throughout the match. And, not about his pathetic excuse for a golf game.

His problem was quite simple, quite predictable, and extremely common. After three decades of marriage, Georgie just wasn't gettin' any. He was none too pleased about it, either.

While still very much in love with his wife, George proved no match for Stephanie's dominant personality. From the earliest days of their marriage, his desire to have as much sex as possible was superseded by Stephanie's desire to have as little as possible. Rarely did George prevail.

The situation deteriorated to the point of desperation, most notably over the last couple of years. What little sexual contact there was became nonexistent.

After listening to George bitch and complain for eighteen straight holes, it occurred to James that there may be a way to solve both of their problems at once...

Chapter 50

His key turned in the lock and the door swung open. Angeline was in her proper place, patiently awaiting his arrival. Kneeling flawlessly, she was simply exquisite.

As expected, she was wearing what he selected before hitting the links. It consisted of a leather house collar, sheer bubble-gum-pink panties, nipple clamps, and mile-high heels. After some consideration, James deemed something askew and had added a sterling silver bell to each clamp.

Stepping back, he'd proudly pronounced them perfect. Not only did the bells complement her skin tone, they completed her ensemble seamlessly. The tinkling at her tits from even the tiniest tremor was music to his ears.

With full intent, James neglected to appraise Angeline of George's unexpected visit. At the sight of the surprise guest, the tolling of the bells surged exuberantly. Her chest heaved as she gasped in shock, breasts joggling. Her breathing escalated to the status of panting.

Those were the only outward sign of dismay. Angeline remained in position; back straight, tits pushed out, and eyes cast down. To this day, James couldn't decide who'd been more stunned, she or old Georgie. Much later, George confided that in his wildest fantasies, he never imagined being greeted by a naked woman on her knees!

The consummate host, James escorted the goggle-eyed magistrate to a comfortable armchair in the front room. Solicitously, he adjusted it, making certain there was a clear view to the delectable sight that was Angeline.

Making his way to the kitchen, he emerged with two beers, passing by Angeline as though she were invisible. Rejoining his buddy, they discussed the highlights and low lights of the day's play. For the sake of accuracy, only James discussed golf. George, beginning to perspire, was either ignoring him—or rendered deaf and dumb.

Blind, however, he was not. Slack-jawed, he guzzled his beer. At the same time, he devoured the clamped and collared vision before him with glazed, unblinking eyes.

Chapter 51

Masturbating vigorously beside a slumbering Missy, James conjured the details of that long ago day as if it were yesterday.

Effortlessly, he recalled the comical look on George's mottled face when Angeline was summoned to 'come'. He'd had real concerns that he might stroke out. More so when she rose obligingly from her heels onto all fours and crawled gracefully towards them.

With that vision dancing in his head, the momentum of James' hand increased as he worked his now-granite dick. Angeline had settled herself precisely where he'd indicated: between George's opened legs. He'd observed as shock blossomed in her eyes, dread on its heels. Conversely, understanding and gratitude shone from George's saucer-wide peepers.

It never once occurred to James that Angeline might balk at his directive and refuse. True, her ongoing ineptitude sorely tested his patience. Not to mention his belt, hand, crop, flogger, paddle, and wooden spoon. Yet, even with her persistent lack of cock sucking fervor, he knew she would never think to disrespect him.

He'd casually instructed Angeline to unzip George's green plaid golf pants and draw forth both his cock *and* his balls. After a micro-second's hesitation, she followed the instructions to the letter. Blatant distaste was naked on her face as she fumbled about in George's plus-fours.

Once the repulsive mandate was accomplished, she was not permitted to take her eyes from the puny, wrinkled genitalia before her. It rested limply atop an unruly mass of gray pubic hair. James remembered her face turning the same shade of green as George's pants.

"Consider this your final tutorial, darling. As you can see, Mr. Weatherly is not as well-endowed as your Master. This affords us the opportunity to improve not only your appreciation, but your technique as well."

"I know how much you desire to please me. Today, I afford you the opportunity to do just that."

Angeline's jaw dropped in disbelief.

"That's it, angel, open wide. Now, might I suggest we get on with it?"

Jerking his rampant, leaking cock, James knew it wouldn't be long now. With Missy sleeping soundly beside him, he was on the verge of exploding for the second time that day. He could almost feel Angeline's soft hair in his hand as he helped himself to a handful. Utilizing the new-found leverage, he'd pressed her face directly into George's uncircumcised groin.

Her dumbfounded gasp was stifled when she'd found herself buried nose-deep in scrotum. The stench of piss and eighteen holes of golf accosted her nostrils.

While he couldn't know it at the time, it was at this juncture that Angeline came to realize the error of her ways. She became infuriated with herself for disappointing James in this most basic of submissive disciplines. With her face buried in another man's groin, she'd determined then and there to make him proud. She'd just realized how incredibly lucky she was.

His hand in her hair became an unnecessary adornment. Awkward but eager, Angeline swallowed the stiffening cock to the root. George's eyes rolled back in their sockets. A groan escaped his lips as time and time again, her hot mouth engulfed him. His gray pubis stabbed at her enlarged lips with every energetic downward stroke.

Observing, James assessed her performance, execution, and enthusiasm. He alternated between hard-edged correction and soothing encouragement.

"Very nice, princess. Now, let's not forget the ball sac. That's it—nice, long, respectful strokes, just as if it were mine."

Angeline suckled at one fleshy teste, then the other, lapping at both noisily. Poor George. Angeline's new and improved technique was almost too effective. His fingers gripped the arms of the chair so tightly, James wondered if they might pierce the fabric. His butt was lifted clear off the seat. His head was thrown back, mouth agape.

Barely begun, this was very close to being over. James spoke to the back of Angeline's bobbing head.

"You're making your Master so proud, angel. Now, be a good girl and lick around the head. We wouldn't want to waste all that delicious pre-cum. You're doing such a good job, my love, that you deserve a reward. You may swallow him to the nuts and open your throat to receive a nice load of jism!"

James was very near to blowing his load as he remembered Angeline with George's cock stuffed down her throat. Inciting her to even loftier heights, he'd reminded her to swallow every drop of her imminent reward.

James' balls tightened, erupting in perfect unison with George, albeit a dozen years later. As one, they came to the sights and sounds of Angeline's award winning display of cock sucking. Covered in snot and drool, she gurgled and grunted as she wolfed down every drop of George's jism.

After licking the softened phallus clean, she'd looked up to her Master. Wearing nothing but a proud smile, her face shone with spit and exertion. There wasn't a single dribble of cum...

Chapter 52

After jerking off into his hand, James rolled over to spoon Missy. Utterly sated, deflated, and already half asleep, he reached around to cup both of her soft breasts in his cum-filled palm. As he rubbed the warm cream into her bulbous nipples, she unconsciously ground her bottom into his sticky cock. James resisted the deep, dreamless slumber that beckoned. Instead, he took a moment to recall the happy ending enjoyed by all that memorable day so long ago.

He knew George's sentiments when an entire case of Remy Martin XO cognac was delivered to his door. The courier driver rang the doorbell twice before proceeding to test the veracity of the knocker. Ultimately, he was forced to leave the pricey liqueur exposed and vulnerable on the front landing.

It's not that James wasn't home. He was. In fact, he was sitting in the front room, in the same chair George had occupied just the previous day. He watched contentedly through the window as the courier's truck pulled away.

At his feet, Angeline was giving him the finest blow-job of his entire life.

Chapter 53

Missy's naked breasts felt as though they were glued together. Bewildered, she reached between them to discover a thick, sticky pool of what could only be semen. It had seeped to the underside of her left tit. She could peel it like a masque from both glazed nipples.

She didn't have a clue as to when or how it was deposited. Given the surreal events of late, a momentary cerebral power failure wasn't out of the question. Was it possible she just didn't remember?

Setting the mystery aside for now, she wallowed in the musky scent of her now-official Master. She inhaled him into her lungs as she stretched from head to toe. The movement drew immediate and sharp attention to her bottom. Inflamed and throbbing, it hotly protested the attention James had lavished upon it earlier. *Upon it and in it!* Traces of his seed still leaked from the dilated orifice.

Whore!

Missy's bladder was full to the danger zone. Mindful not to wake him, she pulled the covers back and slid from the bed. Tip-toeing from the room, she wondered why they'd wound up in his office instead of his bedroom. Caressing the stiff leather collar that marked her as his, she knew it was only a matter of time.

She navigated the unfamiliar hallway as best she could, noticing several closed doors along the way. Finally, she arrived at the tastefully appointed powder room, and not a moment too soon. She almost didn't make it onto the toilet before her bladder let loose its contents in a furious stream.

She couldn't help remembering her first visit to these

very facilities. The erotic recollection hit her full force. Were it a physical blow, she'd have been knocked clean off the toilet. As it was, Missy flushed scarlet from head to toe and back again.

In her mind's eye, she watched in horror as James squatted between her knees. With slow deliberation, he'd spread them wide, and then, wider still. Powerless to break eye contact, her bladder voided mere inches from where he knelt. His satisfied grin spoke volumes.

That little episode had left her faint and amazed. Now, it elicited the identical response, undiminished by the passage of time. Missy anticipated that it would continue to do so for the remainder of her days.

Flushing, she re-traced her steps down the dimly lit hallway. Already, she missed his physical presence. However, now that her distended bladder was dealt with, she found her curiosity piqued by the series of closed doors.

She didn't think he'd mind if...

Chapter 54

Her sixth sense jangled ominously the moment her fingers made contact with the knob.

The first door she opened accessed a musty games room that looked as if it hadn't been used, or dusted, in years. Somehow, Missy knew that *this* room was none so benign. Ignoring her instincts, she turned the knob and peeked in. Her first thought was that James must have a roommate.

In her soul, she knew better.

The large, masculine suite was filled with photos of a woman. And, not just any woman. Quite possibly, this was the most beautiful woman she'd ever laid eyes on. She was everywhere, exquisitely framed on walls and dressers. The room was practically a shrine.

The woman looked to be around Missy's age. She was blessed with a translucent complexion, piercing blue eyes, and masses of strawberry blonde hair. Her soulful eyes appeared to mirror Missy's own, seeming to appraise her just as she speculated at their ethereal beauty.

Gooseflesh rose on her arms and her scalp. She hugged herself, but continued to shiver. She knew she was standing in James' bedroom. There was no doubt that this female was singularly special to him.

Missy's knees gave out from under her. She would have collapsed had she not caught the edge of the dresser. She leaned her full weight against it, dazed. Her head was spinning and her eyes were burning. She was at a complete loss regarding a viable course of action.

This can't be happening!

Gasping for breath, her eyes scanned the room. It was

spotless, not a single mote of dust. It smelled familiarly of cigars and cologne. The once-beloved aromas now caused her throat to clog. She struggled in vain to hold back the tears.

Weeping, she noticed there was a place for everything, and everything was in its place. *Everything—except for that.* A photo album sat smack in the middle of an incredible four-poster bed. With a sick feeling of dread in her gut, she was drawn toward it, helpless to resist.

Opening it, she knew immediately she'd made a huge mistake. While there were no date or time stamps, all the photos appeared fairly recent to Missy's teary eyes. Most were of the woman and James gazing lovingly at each other. In others, they were part of a small group, all smiling happily into the camera.

Is that Stephanie and George?

When she got to images of the gorgeous woman posed in a variety of submissive postures, Missy was grateful for the stream of tears that distorted her vision. Clawing at the newly-bestowed collar, she fled, leaving the album open and tear-stained on the bed.

Bent double in the hallway, her focus was narrowed to the size of a pinprick. Two equally critical mandates reverberated in her brain. One was to catch her breath before she fainted of hyper-ventilation.

The other was to get the hell out of there!

Missy tiptoed past the bed where James snored undisturbed and oblivious. Without a sound, she inched open the top drawer of the desk. It took only a moment to locate and extract the key.

It felt eerily as though she was observing herself from a distance. She remembered the first time she experienced the odd phenomenon. Ironic, how the identical sensation could mark a promising beginning as well as a tragic ending.

The only sound to penetrate the din in her head was the deadbolt sliding free. Hands trembling, she carefully placed the lock on the desk. Noiselessly retracing her steps, she abandoned the once-precious collar at the front door as she raced naked to her car.

Inside, she dropped her head onto the steering wheel and keened out her anguish. How was she going to get home in this condition? Missy made a Herculean effort to steady her quavering emotions. Concentrating on interjecting deep-breathing techniques between hiccups, she somehow managed to start the engine. With one last cleansing breath, she was negotiating the winding driveway, headed towards the main road.

When it dawned on her what James would discover come morning, Missy had no choice. She pulled the Infinity to the curb, again reduced to wretched, gasping sobs...

Chapter 55

The sun took a first, tentative peek over the horizon just as Missy pulled into her driveway. She was naked, nauseated and numb. She was also, miraculously, still in one piece after fleeing James' house in what could only be described as blinding hysterics.

Twelve days later, she was actually nurturing the near-catatonic state of shock that dogged her. It was easier than the alternative, which involved erratic vacillation between love, hate—and sheer bewilderment. Ultimately, as one tortured day melted into the next, Missy settled on hate. Or, so she deluded herself into believing.

Make that hate and chocolate. No matter what, life was just that much easier to digest when chocolate was incorporated. The combination seemed to make James' untenable deception minutely less unbearable.

She wracked her brain wondering about the beautiful blonde. More excruciating was the question of why her image held sway over what was supposed to be *her* Master's chambers. There was no room for quibbling. She presided uncontested over that most privileged of realms.

Scalding shame gripped Missy for the umpteenth time. While *that* creature waited patiently in his boudoir, she was being taken anally—*in his office!* Recalling the Collaring Ceremony, she cringed. Disgrace collaborated with self-doubt, a now-familiar merger.

Overjoyed, she'd tilted her head back to accept his collar, her heart bursting. Her bowels were also bursting—*from a huge deposit of his ejaculate.*

It was around this point that the self-flagellation would

begin anew. Had she the slightest inkling...

Days had passed before the swelling and tenderness of that most sordid deed began to recede. Denial became Missy's closest ally when it dawned that, on some level—she missed the raw sensation.

Whore!

Indeed, she refused to even contemplate the exceptional orgasm she partook of during the depraved act itself. She was far too busy gorging on anger and self-pity to be traumatized by that singularly gut-churning detail!

Why hasn't he called? The question tormented her, ripping through her brain like a bullet.

Why hasn't he come for her? She could no longer deceive herself. There was only one possible explanation. There *was* another woman. No doubt, another submissive woman.

The nausea returned, as it did every time she reflected on what lurked behind that cursed door. A door as outwardly innocuous as any other.

There wasn't so much as a whisper from James in nearly two weeks. The brutality of this left little to be said and less to be done. Unwittingly, she'd found out his secret. Since then, his choice was both clear and appalling.

On this particular day, anger managed to trump desolation. On this particular day, Missy conquered the tears and the nausea by reminding herself of one simple fact.

His choice lay elsewhere...

Chapter 56

After three years of dormancy, James' libido was reawakened with a vengeance. The instant he'd discerned Missy's profoundly submissive nature, the long months of hibernation came to an almost embarrassingly abrupt end.

Similarly, her sudden departure did nothing to diminish it. As his mind labored to accept that she was lost to him, his cock had yet to receive the memo!

"Mister Cole-tun, sir, with that lean phy-sique ya surely don't need any mo' cah-dio!"

It was Jenny Dean, his personal trainer from years gone by. Jenny didn't speak, per se, she squealed. Every southern-dipped word that came out of her mouth was at a damaging, deafening decibel. James was sure she provoked hounds to howl and fillings to throb.

Aside from this one unsettling trait, Jenny was a sweet girl. A sweet girl endowed with a killer body. Sweeter still? Jenny Dean wasn't the least bit conflicted about bestowing that body unto others. A personal trainer and self-proclaimed free spirit, Jenny didn't weigh herself down with mundane niceties such as panties. Or morals.

The spandex micro-shorts she favored were consistently *this* much too short and *that* much too snug. In other words: perfect. Little wonder that her clientele consisted almost entirely of happy, horny, and suspiciously unfit males.

Today, that description suited James to a T. More or less. He sure as hell wasn't happy and he sure as hell wasn't unfit. But horny? *That*, he sure as hell was. And seemingly, without respite.

James noted that he hadn't a single fantasy of his long-deceased wife since that fateful night with Missy. Yet, on that night, Angeline's stunning visage had embedded itself adamantly in his cortex and cooed irresistibly to his genitals.

He'd awoken hard and horny next to a sleeping Missy, but jerked off to memories of Angeline. His sense was that Angeline had known that he was leaving her in the past—her rightful place. He speculated whether she might have played some devious role in Missy's untimely discovery, as well.

James was a realist, not prone to flights of fancy. Still, he was not cavalier enough to rule out all possibilities. Including that of other-worldly. Was it simply a coincidence that on the same day he planned to pack away every tactile memory of Angeline—Missy stumbled across her? When he found his bedroom door ajar and the photo album opened on the rumpled bed, he could only imagine Missy's tormented confusion.

Yet, to his Dominant mind the facts remained clear. She should have come to him with her findings and her feelings. How easily he could have assuaged her fears. How innocent the explanation for Angeline's image adorning his walls. For the first time, he would have shared with another human being his burden of guilt and loss. He would have been candid about his belief that Angeline was the love of his life.

That is, until he'd met Missy!

Yes, he could have put her fears to rest. But, alas, Missy had chosen a different path. One which was inexcusable in his domain. As a result, they would both suffer the consequences of her actions.

There appeared no remedy for the gaping wound to his

soul. It grew larger with every passing day.

Chapter 57

Missy raced back to the vanilla world as fast as her long legs would carry her. She did not dawdle nor did she meander. In fact, she all-out sprinted. No matter that her previous existence within the confines of polite society was exactly that: an existence.

Living, she'd only recently discovered, was something completely different.

Submissive...

Nevertheless, Missy was resolute. She meant to pound the square peg that was her nature into the round, uncompromising hole that was society. She was determined to never again venture from that straight, narrow, and predictable path. Not even a smidgen!

Most errors in judgment turn out to be valuable life lessons. One took them in stride and moved forward, hopefully the wiser. However, there was another kind of misstep, the kind that has the ability to rip out ones innards. James was such a misstep.

His uninterrupted silence screamed with an intensity that words could never equal. It echoed in her skull until Missy thought her head might explode. In truth, she half hoped that it would. Anything to ease the pain.

She told herself that fatigue was to blame for her undoing that day at the grocery store, nothing more. James just happened to be in the right place at the right time to catch her unawares. *Yes, that was it!* She could, and would prevent it from happening again.

Industrial sized reinforcements for that damnable 'closet' door were called for. She would see to it. In short order, life would be back to normal.

That was her story and she so wanted to stick to it.

Unfortunately, no matter how often Missy hammered these self-deceptions into her head, they remained stubbornly unsustainable in her heart. That traitorous organ throbbed for James every single moment of every single day. Unimpressed with the ramblings of a mind deep in denial, it clung obstinately to the truth.

Emotionally drawn and quartered, she hated him all the more.

Still, his silence seemed glaringly inconsistent with his previous words. He spoke so convincingly of honor, of responsibility—of self-accountability.

And yet...

Lately, there were tortured, sleepless nights. More and more often, Missy caught herself wondering if she was missing something. Something important. True, she should never have snooped. It was wrong to enter rooms in his house without permission. But, considering what she'd discovered, surely his epic deceit superseded her minor trespass?

Did it not?

She told herself that the bigger miscalculation was falling in love with a two-timing charlatan with an overpowering personality and a gifted tongue.

A *very* gifted tongue.

Missy sighed. She would not waver. She could not waver...

Chapter 58

James was pouring sweat.

Abusing the already overworked elliptical machine, he glanced down at the brightly lit display panel. It flashed and buzzed in exhausted surrender, as if pleading with him to cease and desist. Forty minutes now, and yet, his frustration was far from slackened.

James swiped at the sweat burning his eyeballs and increased his pace. It happened then, unbidden. Missy besieged his thoughts, disrupting his composure for the umpteenth time. His mind insisted on dredging up that forgettable morning on which he awoke to find her gone. The only remnant was her scent. It had taunted him from sheets still damp with her sweat.

She'd left one other item behind. The collar. He specifically recalled the pain of retrieving it from the floor where she'd discarded it like trash.

His already punishing pace quickened yet again. James missed her more than he would admit, even to himself. Still, no matter how fast or how often he ran, the indisputable facts remained fixed. Missy showed herself to be unworthy.

James increased his speed.

He'd gone to great lengths to ensure she understood the symbolic import of being collared. Explained in detail the almost ritualistic aspects attached to its acceptance. And its removal. Taking it off without his knowledge or permission was in itself insupportable. Throwing it onto the floor compounded the insult tenfold. The two actions combined spawned the super glue that sealed both their fates.

His thoughts were shattered by his personal trainer's

piercing voice.

"How 'bout y'all come down now an' do a few push-ups with me, Mr. Cole-tun?"

James figured that Jenny must have been more than a little surprised when he called to set up this training session. The first time they'd worked together was about three years ago, not long after Angeline's death. While she came highly recommended, he'd canceled the balance of ten non-refundable sessions after just four.

Jenny, having no idea of the black hole in which he'd existed at the time, made it blatantly clear that she was interested in pumping much more than just his biceps. He was in a bad way then, and wasn't one to share his feelings.

Today, he was burdened with no such qualms. When at last he dismounted the smoking elliptical, James mounted an even hotter Jenny. When one's personal trainer recommended a few push-ups, one did not dispute her professional advice. However, instead of performing the muscle-building calisthenic beside her, James chose to execute them atop of her!

One thing Jenny Dean wasn't was shy. She began to wriggle, jiggle, and giggle her carnal objectives the moment the door swung open in greeting. Every honey-dipped word that came out of her luscious mouth was sugar-coated with sexual innuendo.

Always the self-sacrificing host, James aimed to please – and his aim was right on target. Jenny's acquiescence consisted of a single, skull splitting squeal. He wasted little time on formalities. Positioning her on all fours, he didn't bother to take down the tiny micro-shorts. Yanking the cooperative material to one side he tested the waters, finding them warm and at high tide.

Clamping one hand over Jenny's shrieking mouth, James dove right in...

Chapter 59

Missy came fully awake with a jolt and an objective. Her mind felt well-rested and sharp for the first time in what seemed an eternity.

Today, she was going to find out exactly who that woman was. No matter that she hadn't seen or heard from James in over a month. The not knowing was haunting her nights and tormenting her days.

It was more than just morbid curiosity that motivated her, however. She'd always trusted her gut, and typically, followed its guidance. In truth, she credited it with saving her life, more than once. Yet, it was this same sixth sense which had screamed out for her to believe in James. To trust in him without reservation. Missy needed to understand, if she was to have faith in herself ever again.

The events of that morning had devastated her to the point of leaving protective gaps in her memory. As time passed, the gaps slowly closed. Today, she'd been jarred awake when one virtually snapped shut: *It had been Stephanie in that picture!* Stephanie would know who the woman was.

Missy brewed fresh coffee and forced herself to ingest calories in the form of a blueberry muffin smothered with butter. She was infused with energy and direction. Today, there was a mission to accomplish. Missy was like a dog with a bone.

While speaking with Stephanie was paramount, it wasn't the sole reason for visiting Ebony&Ivory today. Also on the agenda was talking to Teresa about getting her job back.

The twenty-five thousand dollar check that James gave

Christopher was a godsend, for sure. Almost half a year's worth of her wages with just a few casual swirls of his chi-chi fountain pen. Still, with Christopher heading off to college, it wouldn't last forever.

By the time Missy arrived at the boutique it was half past ten and the place was hopping. Stephanie, Teresa, and Carla, a part-time employee, were all occupied with at least one customer apiece. The regal door chimes heralded her arrival. Two beleaguered employees and their boss glanced up as one.

As their respective customers were complimented, coddled, and escorted out, the girls welcomed Missy with warm hugs and kiss-kisses on both cheeks. Teresa was first to speak. She was holding both of Missy's hands, her eyes appraising.

"Missy, darling, you've lost weight. You look simply mah-velous!"

In truth, Missy looked the furthest thing from *mah-velous*. Her complexion was pale and her cheeks were hollow, in direct contrast to her clothing which bagged on her shrinking frame. Recalling that Teresa adhered to the age-old adage that a woman could never be too rich or too thin, Missy smiled and thanked her ex-boss for the sweet compliment. It was Teresa's next words which caused any remaining color to drain from Missy's face.

"So, do tell, Missy dear. How is that sexy man of yours?"

Chapter 60

"Little one?"

Missy knew who it was before the familiar endearment was so much as uttered. She knew before her five tactile senses could begin to correlate and assess the data. She felt this man in the very core of her soul.

She realized then and there that her most dedicated attempt to extricate him from her thoughts would be in vain. He consumed her utterly. There could be no further denial, no further justification. Resistance was, and had always been —futile.

Master...

As was usual in his presence, everything else fell away as trivial and irrelevant. All that remained were the two of them. Man and woman. Master and adoring whore.

With Teresa's blessing, Stephanie was taking an early and extended lunch break. Leaving Missy's jalopy in the staff lot, they'd hopped into Steph's silver Lexus hybrid. They decided to head over to the nearby shopping center and grab a bite to eat.

Chitting and chatting with their heads close together, they meandered down the mall in the direction of the food court. Oblivious to their surroundings, they were forced to a jarring halt when Missy suddenly collided with something solid and unyielding.

Solid, unyielding, and with just a hint of distinctive cologne and designer cigar. Missy's instincts did not require collaboration. There could be no mistake.

His hands still gripped her arms where they steadied her upon impact. The heat created permeated her clothing, warmed her body, and seared her heart. She couldn't have said whether she wanted him to leave them there forever—or remove them at once. She also couldn't determine whether the erratic heartbeat pounding in her ears was hers, his—or theirs. It took every ounce of constraint she could muster to not reach out and touch him.

"You look thin, pet."

His soothing, hypnotic voice washed over and through her. His eyes pierced to the heart of her. There was no question. She *was* his pet. Missy was exactly where she was born to be: near him. With a mouth as dry as sandpaper and a tongue that felt cumbersome and foreign, she somehow managed to respond.

"As do you, sir."

It was true. Her heart broke as she took in his leaner physique. She suppressed a bizarre desire to lick at the dark smudges beneath his eyes. In her blind adoration, Missy was sure she could eradicate them.

Too soon, his hands fell away from her shoulders and the spell was broken. He turned the full brunt of his attention, which was formidable, on Stephanie. Bending at the waist to gallantly kiss the back of her hand, he asked after his old friend George.

James listened politely as the almost sixty year old woman gulped and giggled her way through a blushing response. He then bid them a sudden adieu, citing a meeting he was already late for. With only a cursory nod in Missy's direction, he turned and disappeared into the crowd. She was positive somebody had just punched a hole in her heart.

She could actually feel the air escaping her body...

Chapter 61

With a bag of Cheezies and a wine glass in one hand, an uncorked bottle in the other, Missy collapsed into the cushions of her well-worn sofa. Determined to focus on sweet nothingness, she switched on the television and turned up the volume. Hopefully, the white noise would rise above the turmoil that was clamoring for attention in her skull.

Drained and disheartened from an overwhelming day, she tore into the bag of chips and poured herself a glass of wine. Throwing etiquette to the wind, she filled the glass nearly to over flowing. With the utmost of caution, she raised it to her lips. Without spilling a single drop, Missy noisily slurped off enough to lower the contents to a more manageable level.

And then, she filled it again.

Cheezies, Anderson Cooper, and vino for din-din? Missy figured a girl could do worse. Giggling at her own hilarity, she was already well on the way to tipsy. Not a difficult sojourn, considering the only thing in her stomach was knots and bile. It had been impossible to maintain any appetite for lunch. It was gone the moment she ran into James, along with her breath and all good sense.

The flesh of her upper arms still burned where his hands had supported her. It provided her only source of warmth. She shivered in reaction to the potency of that unexpected contact.

Yet, he'd simply walked away.

Stephanie, as usual, was watching her weight. Missy couldn't help but smile, watching her dig into a salad that probably boasted more calories than a platter of pasta in cream sauce. It soon became clear, however, that Steph was far more interested in what just transpired between James and Missy than anything on her plate.

"Little one? Pet? *sir?*"

She repeated the strange endearments, enunciating the next with more indignation than the last.

"What the heck was that all about, *little* Miss Missy?"

Blushing crimson, Missy tried to pass off the unusual terminology as simply their way of expressing fondness and mutual respect. Calling him sir just seemed so natural.

Master...

Unimpressed and unappeased, blatant curiosity was written all over Stephanie's face. Seeing it, Missy was grateful, at least, that she hadn't uttered the word 'Master'. She winced, imagining Steph's apoplectic expression if that were the case!

Desperate to change the highly sensitive subject, Missy disclosed a tidbit almost as juicy.

"It didn't work out between us, Steph. I was in way over my head. Not to mention how obvious it is that he's just fine without me."

Shaken by the brutal truth of the statement, she promptly shifted the discussion back to Angeline before she began to bawl. Her toasted bacon, lettuce, and tomato sandwich sat untouched before her.

At least now the face had a name to match. *Angeline.*

As it turned out, the photos were much older than Missy originally assumed. Or imagined, thanks to her frenzied state at the time. Stephanie figured them to be about a dozen years old. Thinking back, she remembered that she and George had socialized with James and Angeline on only a couple occasions. Both times, they were part of a larger group.

If she recalled correctly, they were engaged to be married at the time, and Stephanie was sure that grand event did occur. While she remembered Angeline as young, beautiful and sophisticated, she could not recall sharing a single conversation with her.

"What I do remember is George ogling her to the point of making a complete fool of himself. He behaved like a besotted teenager, the old goat. Can you imagine anything more ridiculous?"

The two women chuckled at the notion as they exited the mall arm-in-arm. With her mind planted firmly in the past, Stephanie abruptly stopped laughing.

"I believe she passed away a few years back."

Missy's legs felt like rubber. Sucker-punched, she barely managed to climb into the flashy Lexxus.

Now, slumped on her couch and already more than a teensy bit intoxicated, Missy Weaver gave up all hope of losing herself in the sweet nothingness she aspired to. She decided instead to lose herself in another glass of wine.

I ran from a ghost...

Chapter 62

That son of a bitch knew damned well it was an illegal drop! Two-shot penalty, my ass! Disqualify the cheating prick!

James Colton was two things: in a black mood and no fan of Tiger Woods. He had little respect for any man who couldn't keep his putter in his pants. In fact, one of his favorite maxims was: Males like him give men like me a bad name.

On the other hand, James loved the game of golf. Today, it was a re-run of the 2013 Masters Championship. Reclining in his favorite chair with his favorite cigar, he was watching his favorite sport. James knew he ought to be counting his many blessings.

Fuck, I miss her...

He was also aware that he ought to delineate between Tiger's professional and personal life. In Tiger's case, however, he made a conscious decision to not. It irked him that misogyny on such a grandiose scale could be swept under the rug, or in this case—under the perfectly manicured green. Just a few key *strokes* later, and a hobbled society cheers. James almost snorted in derision at the irony.

He knew of far more happily-ever-after Dominant/submissive relationships than he did mainstream, or 'vanilla'. His marriage was an excellent example, despite it being cut tragically short. Many women professed to never feeling more alive or more fulfilled than after emerging from the damnable closet.

She looked so thin...

There is an inherent grace and freedom in submission. From it blossoms a deep sense of accomplishment. Similarly, self-control and responsibility are inherent in the very essence of the word 'Dominant'. Anything less is a glaring sign of fraudulence, and perhaps, even danger.

She didn't trust me...

Respect also plays a crucial role and is *not* a one-way street. Contrary to popular opinion, the submissive component of the relationship is a full and contributing half, nothing less. By definition, one is incomplete without the other. To be sure, what is a Dom without his sub? Conversely, what is a bottom without her Top?

Why would she throw it all away without so much as a word?

Sure, society gasps in scandalized horror when confronted with words such as slut, whore, or heaven forbid, cunt. Yet, the truth lies behind too many closed doors to count. That's where 'respectable' men everywhere are hurling those exact words at their women. *In anger.*

When two people are free to share their deepest thoughts and most carnal desires without fear of judgment, there remains little need for rage or deceit. While the same words may be commonplace in the BDSM domain, a true Dominant would never utter them in anger. *That* would constitute the epitome of disrespect.

She left me no choice...

Chapter 63

Missy was messed up and she knew it.

Disoriented, she emerged from an alcohol-induced slumber with one arm twisted at an impossible angle beneath her. Now, it hung useless at her side, numb from shoulder to fingertips. A zillion razor-sharp needles pierced the frozen limb as fresh, alcohol-infused blood rushed to its rescue.

Cringing, she braced against the excruciating onslaught of the blaring television. The volume she once welcomed had transformed itself while she dozed. It was now a hot poker buried directly between her throbbing eyeballs!

Peeling one unwilling lid open at a time, the empty wine bottle came into semi-focus. Its lack of contents made it only too apparent why her mouth felt like sandpaper and her head felt like shit.

With both palms flat on the coffee table, Missy managed to get her feet planted beneath her. Hoping for the best but prepared for the worst, she rose ever-so-cautiously to her full stature.

Pleased with her progress, she paused, breathing hard. When the spinning slowed and the nausea settled, she collected the bottle and half-filled glass. Stumbling to the kitchen, she dumped the dregs down the sink. Missy swore she would never, ever drink again.

On second thought, she couldn't imagine a better day to get wasted. It sucked to begin with, hurtling downhill from there. It was nothing short of grueling; forced to watch as James strode away ever so casually. Whereas he seemed unaffected by their chance encounter, Missy was left virtually gutted.

It got worse still after learning she'd been jealous of a ghost. A memory. Her odious behavior that fateful day was reminiscent of a spoiled brat who hadn't gotten what she'd wanted for Christmas. How she wished she'd given James the benefit of the doubt and simply asked for an explanation.

Still, it wasn't until she and Stephanie returned to the boutique that the final nail was hammered into the coffin that best embodied her day. Teresa unwittingly did the honors, informing Missy that her old job was no longer available. Carla was promoted to full-time, and another part-timer was just hired.

Utterly defeated, Missy was only peripherally aware when Teresa changed the topic. *Why was she talking about Ethan Montgomery?* Accustomed to getting whatever, and whomever he desired, Ethan was pestering Teresa about Missy. Since her blatant rejection, his interest hadn't abated as one might expect. Au contraire, it seemed strangely whetted.

How did he not find their first date as unbearable as she remembered? Slouched drunkenly against the kitchen sink, Missy retched, making a conscious decision to blame the wine. Fate had thrown her into James' arms. They'd embraced her with a strength wrought of understanding and a heat borne of recognition. She wasn't at all certain she could go on without their embrace.

In slow motion, she again dissected every gut-wrenching detail as he turned from her and walked away. Each step he took stomped on the fragile thread of hope to which she clung. She could deceive herself no longer. It was time to face facts and rejoin the real world.

Missy retched again. This time, there could be no blaming the wine...

Chapter 64

You're a fucking idiot is what you are!

Scowling at the mirror, James spoke directly at his own reflection. He was dealing with his hurt and frustration over Missy's exodus as would any normal, red-blooded male. He called Jenny. The Southern fried personal trainer shrilled in eager acceptance of his unscheduled invitation. He made no mention of working out and she didn't ask. There was no mistaking the type of *session* he expected today.

Stepping out from an impossibly hot shower, James wrapped a towel around his waist and grinned at his clever play on words. At least, it felt like a grin. One glance in the vapor-streaked mirror exposed the truth. What he thought was a smile was actually a grotesque scowl. James couldn't remember the last time he'd smiled.

Also problematic was the fact that only his genitals were in need of feminine attention. His mind, detached and indifferent, roamed freely. Without a second thought, it made a beeline straight for Missy.

That infuriating woman is going to be the death of me!

As days turned into weeks turned into months, James transitioned from infuriated to desolate, and back again. Eventually, he'd settled on just plain wretched. The ache in his heart and the emptiness in his soul were not lessening with the passage of time.

The time had come to face facts and do something about the untenable state of affairs. He'd spent three ghastly years pining for his deceased wife. He refused to squander one more precious day. Especially over what boiled down to pigheadedness over a damned ritual. He cursed his decision to let Missy go uncontested. What was he thinking? Self-aware, James realized that his ego played a larger part in the fiasco than he cared to admit.

True, he tried to impress upon her the inherent responsibilities attached to being collared. Unfortunately, he gave no consideration to her inexperience. Worse, he offered no leeway in recognition of that naiveté.

It was his duty to guide and instruct. Instead, he'd dealt her a garbage hand then called her feeble bluff. The only 'out' she'd had was through the front door!

Toweling off, James reminded himself to check his condom supply. Jenny was a 'friendly' girl. *Very* friendly. She was referred to James by one of her many satisfied clients, as that client was referred before him. And so it went with free spirited Jenny. Like he said, friendly.

Satisfied that he was loaded for bear—or Jenny—in the condom department, he quickly prepared for his booty call. And, what a booty it was. In his mind, James conjured the last time Jenny visited. It was a wham, bam, thank you ma'am type of engagement—which was perfect, much like her ass. Judging by her wide grin and flushed cheeks, he could only surmise she left equally as gratified.

James was planning an encore performance this evening. One act. No curtain calls. Jenny Dean would be exiting, stage right, before the lights were raised!

Chapter 65

With seven hundred and fifty milliliters of alcohol as encouragement, immersing herself in self-pity was an uncomplicated endeavor.

Missy was disgusted with life in general, specifically—her own. She decided she'd endured enough crap for one day. Head and heart throbbing, she chased a couple of aspirins with a couple of handfuls of lukewarm water. Taking a deep breath, she steeled herself for the last leg of the day's excruciating journey.

When she was able to stand without the kindly assistance of the kitchen counter, she did so with care. Lightheaded, Missy began the perilous trek down the hallway that led to nirvana, otherwise known as her bed. She was so close to sweet oblivion, she could taste it.

Lurching past Christopher's room, it struck her how much she missed him. He and two buddies had driven up to check out the new campus. The plan was to share off-campus living quarters and expenses. It was comforting to know they'd have each other.

Still, the idea of her baby living away caused tears to well in her bloodshot eyes and loneliness to creep into her broken heart. Where had the years gone?

Overcome with a sudden longing to be closer to her son, Missy opened his bedroom door and stepped into 'The Cave'. Her senses were immediately flooded with Christopher. While the tears persisted, she felt better already. She glanced around the well-christened lair.

Mountains of scholastic and athletic awards were strewn about haphazardly. Wrinkled posters of half-naked starlets and fast foreign cars hung tattered and askew. Discarded clothing inhabited dark corners.

The books, however, while frayed from use, stood in pristine form and order. From comics to King to Tolstoy, they lined the shelves and much of the floor. The familiar scent of her son pervaded the small space. Missy inhaled deeply.

It was then she saw the computer. It was the old relic that Christopher was forced to upgrade time and time again over the years. They could never quite afford a new one. That is, until recently, when it was replaced courtesy of James' jaw-dropping monetary endowment. Now, the dinosaur sat under a blanket of dust, forgotten.

Missy and computers were incompatible, period. More akin to oil and water than chocolate and peanut butter, her resentment toward them ran deep. Occasionally, Christopher attempted to demonstrate the simplicity of navigating the world-wide-web. It was usually a matter of minutes before they both gave up in exasperation.

And so it was that Missy was equipped with only the most rudimentary capability, and that was fine with her. She could serve a customer and close the boutique. What more did she need? Whereas she usually avoided them at all costs, today she found herself drawn to the technological monstrosity.

Getting to it was no small feat, considering the room's state of disarray and her tenuous claim to sobriety. Nonetheless, she made her way over and around all obstacles, managing to somehow not concuss herself.

Missy sat down in front of a dark screen in the middle of a dark room and wondered what the hell she was doing. In answer, she searched high and low for the 'on' button.

Already annoyed, she hit it accidentally. Something, somewhere, whirred to life. Lights flashed. Music played. The screen lit up and silence prevailed once again.

Now what?

Hesitating only momentarily, Missy placed faltering fingers on the keyboard. Of their own volition, they tapped out a single word.

Submissive...

Chapter 66

Ethan Montgomery III was even more handsome than Missy remembered.

A textbook six foot two with eyes of blue, he came dressed in, what was for him casual attire: nubby beige linen pants, fitted cream colored silk tee, and a custom-cut black sports jacket. Armani, if Missy knew her designers, and she did. He wore his Armani open, nonchalant-like.

Almost before the door swung open, it was obvious that his penchant for cologne was not diminished. Likewise, his propensity for opulent jewels was on full and blinding display. Ethan was the poster boy for the old cliché about money not being able to buying good taste. Wedged within the narrow doorway of her modest home, he appeared as displaced as a slick politician in an urban ghetto.

He seemed well aware of the incongruity. Clearly uncomfortable, he shifted his weight from one sleek Italian loafer to the other. One manicured hand held a breathtaking bouquet of midnight blue roses. In the other, a crumpled silk handkerchief. Missy suspected the hankie was implemented to protect his precious knuckles from coming into contact with her shabby door.

Admonishing herself for being a nasty bitch, she smiled sweetly and invited him in. Accepting the proffered bouquet with all the enthusiasm she could muster, she leaned in to kiss his cheek. When he turned his head and caught her lips, Missy did not pull away.

Four days had passed since she'd sat half-baked at her son's computer and discovered the terrible truth. Four days since she came face to face with her unpardonable offense.

The offense she now knew James could never forgive.

The Google search of 'submissive' hadn't revealed anything earth shattering. It served only to verify what she already knew and what she spent a lifetime denying.

Submissive...

Moving on to the broader topic of 'BDSM', Missy unearthed a virtual mountain of information. When at last she turned off the computer, she was sorry she'd ever turned it on. The mountain had turned into a bona fide avalanche. Buried beneath the carnage were Missy and all remaining hope.

It began well enough, she recalled. Wikipedia defined BDSM as '*a variety of erotic practices involving Dominance and submission, role-playing, restraint, power exchange, and other interpersonal dynamics.*' Missy was enthralled to learn that BDSM was an acronym. It denoted the three separate and unique components of the lifestyle.

She had no idea that the letters 'B' and 'D' represented Bondage & Discipline while the 'S' and 'M' referred to Sadism & Masochism, the most extreme derivative of BDSM. The 'D' and 'S' stood for Dominance and Submission.

It was this component that best defined James' perspective. A Dominant/submissive relationship is based on the gift of submission, not the abuse of power. It consists of two equal and opposite parts, the Dom and the sub—often referred to as the Top and bottom. For the most part, the Top leads and the bottom follows. The Top protects, the bottom serves.

In the end, both are fulfilled.

Still, the masses cluck their tongues and shake their heads in self-righteous disapproval. BDSM is deviant and its practitioners freaks, end of discussion. No consideration is given to the countless needs met or souls nourished. In fact, the idiom used within the lifestyle was *'Safe, Sane, and Consensual'*.

Missy laughed out loud when she read that many upstanding representatives of society unknowingly dabble on the fringes of BDSM. Anyone who has ever been blindfolded or had their butt slapped during lovemaking has crossed over into that dark realm.

She scanned through the pages of data, stopping at the section titled *'The Collar.'* It was there she found what she dreaded most. If her heart weren't already broken, it would have shattered again. She read the paragraph a second time, hoping she'd missed some small shred of hope the first. She hadn't.

"The collar signifies the union between a Dominant and his submissive. It is the single most recognizable symbol of a BDSM relationship. Likened to a wedding band, devotees insist its meaning is much more complex. Often, there are private ceremonies to commemorate the event."

"It is never taken lightly and never performed under the influence. It is meant as a commitment to last not only a lifetime, but an eternity. Removal by either party usually signifies the dissolution of the union. Almost invariably, it is irrevocable."

And with that, utter hopelessness engulfed her...

Chapter 67

Missy meant to seduce this man. Fuck his brains out, in fact. Moreover, she was going to enjoy it. Even if it killed her.

And so it was that Missy not only allowed Ethan to kiss her, Missy kissed Ethan back. She kissed him fervently, with real optimism in her heart. She was determined to overcome her slip from the straight and narrow. She frowned at her choice of words. *Slip?* Hardly. Free fall was more like it.

Earlier, she and Ethan talked about going for a bite to eat or maybe taking a stroll through City Park. Exotic flowers from around the globe would be in full bloom at this time of year. Missy, however, had other plans.

She despised the idea of returning to the half-life she'd half-lived before James tore it asunder. Like Humpty Dumpty, it was impossible to put back together again. Tinder to his fire, its layers of protective hypocrisy were nothing but smoldering ash. Only the truth remained.

Submissive...

Still, Missy was counting on the fact that people changed every day if they wanted to badly enough. She reasoned that if one could change from left handed to right, how much harder could it be to just *not* be submissive? All she needed was a little inner fortitude and a plan.

Luckily, Missy had both. When Ethan drew back in shock and disbelief, she became the aggressor, leaning her body seductively into his.

"How about we stay in tonight, Ethan?"

He opened his mouth to respond, but she made it impossible. Her soft tongue slid between his lips and nestled against his. Actions replaced words. He kissed her hard, tongue stiff and darting. They kissed until he broke it off again, gasping for air. If he wasn't sweating when he arrived, he was now.

Unfortunately, Missy felt nothing. Nada. Zilch. It appeared that while her head was on board with her brilliant scheme, her body chose to disregard the memo. It was simply refusing to cooperate. Infuriated with the betrayal, she intensified her efforts.

Taking Ethan's hand, she drew him into her tiny living room and helped him to remove his jacket. She hung it *very* carefully. She proceeded to make him as comfortable as possible on the threadbare sofa. The polite thing would be to offer him a drink. Quite frankly, Missy was afraid her nerve would evaporate in the time it took to pour.

'Polite' was not on the agenda this evening. A piercing scream reverberated in Missy's head. Ignoring it as best she could, she smiled prettily. Holding her breath, she climbed onto Ethan's lap.

From that vantage point, it was a simple matter to straddle his inflamed groin and push her breasts into his panting, perspiring face.

Chapter 68

A piercing scream reverberated in his head. Grimacing against it, James paced the hallways of his house like a caged animal. Something was terribly out of kilter in his universe. He couldn't begin to fathom what it was. He didn't recall ever experiencing such an urgent sense of foreboding. Adrenaline flooded his nervous system in jolts of manic intensity. James was prepared for either fight or flight, whichever was necessary.

And, therein lay the conundrum. Neither was necessary, as far as he knew. James continued to roam the shadowy corridors, anxiety building. Getting nowhere fast, he focused on curbing the escalating apprehension.

Try as he might, he could think of nothing but Missy. He felt her in his heart, tasted her on his lips. He would have sworn that he heard her in his head, as well. It was as though her very essence was reaching out to him, reminiscent of the first day they met. In his mind, he went to her. Making 'contact', James felt a modicum of relief.

Little one...

She was his! To the core and through and through, no matter how much she wished it were otherwise. Blood rushed to his cock at the delectable image of his whore on her knees at his feet. They both knew it was where she belonged.

A Dominant worthy of the title recognizes when he's made a mistake. Arrogance and pettiness were usually beneath him, and yet, James realized he'd succumbed to both. The wrath he'd so stubbornly maintained was painfully unsustainable. He fully acknowledged his culpability. He would have her in her proper place once again. His mind was made up.

With Missy inundating his senses and adrenaline surging useless through his veins, he ceased his pacing and sat down behind his desk. He was determined to not cause her any more misery. On that note, he removed his checkbook from the desk, making good on the second installment he'd promised Christopher. Enlisting a courier company to deliver it without delay, he knew the twenty-five thousand dollars would be deposited into a joint account with his mother. It was earmarked for Christopher's tuition and Missy's peace of mind.

With that piece of business concluded, James realized that the desolate scream in his head had not waned. Nor had the adrenaline ceased to assail his blood stream. He could think of only one practical release.

Making himself comfortable, James began to masturbate...

Chapter 69

Ethan's cock was similar in dimension to James'. At the moment, it was wrapped securely in latex and zealously pumping her Death-Valley-dry pussy.

Missy was desolate. Just the thought of James caused her heart to hammer and her genitals to swell and moisten in response. With Ethan she was ice. Glacial. Numb from the neck down. The same anesthetized sensation she'd experienced with any man other than James. Grasping this sad state of affairs, she prayed the numbness spread to her brain, as well.

She'd promised herself beforehand to not be seduced by thoughts of James. Diligently, she focused on Ethan. He was in great shape, well-muscled and lean. With her eyes squeezed shut, she could barely tell that his skin was the color of irradiated flour. He was so shockingly pale that he literally glowed in the dark.

At least the almost visible wall of cologne had dissipated. Either that or she'd grown accustomed. She wondered if the stench might have triggered the blood-curdling scream that still echoed in her head.

Ethan thrust into her again and again, oblivious to her distress. The friction was becoming unbearable. At least, it was for her. Desperately, Missy worked her own clit, licked dry fingers and tried again. *Nothing.* She was on the verge of faking an orgasm and finishing him off by hand.

It was then that her determination crumbled, followed closely by her defenses. She surrendered wholly to that which she could not control nor modify: her nature. Instantly, James flooded her thoughts, and immediately thereafter—her pussy.

Master...

She was his! To the core and through and through, no matter how fervently he wished it otherwise. She felt him in her heart, tasted him on her lips. It was almost as though she could hear him in her mind.

Missy imagined herself naked at his feet. She was begging clemency for the blatant disrespect she'd exhibited when she cast off his collar and fled without a word. It didn't occur to her that James missed her as much as she did him. All she knew for sure was how badly she wanted him back.

Beneath her, Ethan grunted in rapturous oblivion. In her head, James magically produced the slotted spatula. She remembered it only too well. The strong impression it left on her bottom, and on her psyche, brought an involuntary moan to her lips. The muscles in her pussy convulsed.

All of a sudden, she was engorged with desire. Impaled upon Ethan's cock, Missy found purchase at last and bucked shamelessly against his pubis.

In her mind's eye, James was having her kneel up in order to better present him her breasts. Without hesitation, she lifted her bottom from her heels. His forgiveness would be absolute, but not before she did penance for her insolence. She knew what was coming.

Mentally, she hoisted one teat in each hand, pulling them outward and upward for his convenience.

Whore!

Reality imitated fantasy as thick excretion streamed from her body, drenching Ethan's balls. When the first imaginary stroke of the spatula made contact with the tender flesh of her breast, the white pain took her breath away. Nine more strokes were administered, including two directly to each throbbing nipple. Missy shrieked out a mind-blowing orgasm.

Still heaving from sweet release, she opened her eyes. A shit-eating, ear-to-ear grin greeted her. She'd been vaguely aware of Ethan moaning through an orgasm of his own, now neatly and hygienically collected into a durable, top of the line condom. Apparently, he was assuming full responsibility for her orgasm, as well.

That was fine with Missy. She could never tell him he'd had precious little to do with it. It was James who invaded her mind and commandeered her every sense.

Master...

Chapter 70

Although it irked him to have to utilize his own spit as lubrication, James masturbated vigorously nonetheless. In the short time it took him to teeter on the brink of orgasm, his dick was chafing from the unaccustomed friction.

Still, he perceived that Missy was right there with him. On bended knee, she gazed up at him with love shining from those incredible eyes. While James could happily contemplate their depths for the remainder of his days, there was a more pressing issue at hand. One which was about to explode, in fact!

He visualized her rising from her heels at his request. Imagined her shocked expression when informed that his desire was to blow his load all over her lovely tits. He could almost see the disbelief at his directive to smile pretty whilst holding them proudly forth for his orgasmic pleasure.

There was no need to hold back, and James didn't. He growled his release, coating the distended, if imaginary, orbs in copious amounts of semen.

In reality, of course, he came all over his own belly and thighs. And floor.

Reaching for the box of tissues on his desk, James was mystified as to why, in his mind's eye, Missy's breasts appeared to be covered with welts...

Chapter 71

James dislodged what's-her-name's inch long claws from his thigh and hip checked her around to the far side of the circular booth. He was dining at The Pitts, one of the most popular steakhouses in town. Joining him this evening was His Honorable George T. Weatherly and his most recent *assistant*, Bimbo.

Brenda.

Whatever.

After ejaculating all over himself and an ensuing shower, James remained on edge. He was coming down hard from the inexplicable jolt of adrenaline.

He determined that tomorrow would be the day that he and Missy reunited. He would do whatever was necessary to put this madness behind them. One was only half without the other. He saw the ravages of her suffering the day they'd bumped into each other at the shopping center. As she'd no doubt seen his.

Once back in his loving arms, she would be punished for her transgression, of course. It was just a matter of passing the hours between then and now. James relished the thought of her begging for her well-deserved chastisement, whatever that might be. He would see to it that she thanked him at its conclusion, as well.

Marking that thought, James dug into a choice cut of meat. He was elated to find it seasoned and grilled to perfection. Ravenous, he sawed off another mouthful before swallowing the first, chasing it all down with half a glass of premium red wine. Wiping his lips, he turned his attention to his companions.

Years ago, Judge Georgie underwent a mind-blowing sexual awakening. It had been at the hands, and mouth, of James' deceased wife, Angeline. Apparently, he'd experienced an epiphany as well as an orgasm on that miraculous day. A sex deprived George Weatherly swore he'd never go 'hungry' again. As God was his witness, in fact.

Since then, he was rarely seen without a very young, very blonde paramour. Today, Barbie—er, Brenda, looked to be the approximate age of George's youngest grandchild.

She wiggled her way over to James' side of the table yet again. Yet again, her razor sharp nails imbedded themselves into his thigh. Completing the trifecta, James yet again hip checked her back to George's side of the table.

It was painfully obviously where her interest lay. Luckily, when it came to his *assistants*—George wasn't exactly the jealous type. He made no qualms about it—what was his was James'.

While unable to retain her first name, James was sure that her middle name was Tenacity. Defending against Tenacity's repeated advances was becoming a bit of a challenge. The adrenaline that raced through his bloodstream earlier was quickly turning to sludge. Sapped of strength and energy, he could imagine how it felt to complete an Olympic decathlon. His eyelids began to close of their own accord.

It was then that he saw her. Missy and an attractive older man were just being seated. Their table was directly within his line of vision. If he glanced at George, there was no escaping the smiling couple just beyond.

Couple?

James couldn't remember feeling this hopeless since the day Angeline died in his arms.

Chapter 72

The water washed over her in torrents. Still, Missy dared not close her eyes. She was sure the sight of that trashy bitch hanging all over James was indelibly imprinted on her eyelids. Feeling dirty and deflated, she turned the shower on full blast and punished herself, allowing the piping hot needles to sear her flesh.

After disembarking from Ethan's cock faster than the speed of light, they'd decided to carry on with their previously interrupted plans. Missy was not malicious. She felt terribly that she'd misled him, even if it weren't her intent.

For his part, Ethan insisted on maintaining that asinine 'I da man' smirk long past its expiration date. Missy sighed. She was probably just jealous. She would be on top of the world too had she felt even one shiver of desire for this man.

Deciding to dine at The Pitts, their meals had just arrived when Missy noticed Stephanie's husband, George, approaching their table. Pleasantly surprised to see him, she'd smiled warmly. She was just about to ask after her friend when the rest of his party came into view. Words had abandoned her.

Not for one second did it occur to her that the garish almost-child could be with George.

She couldn't recall a single word of the stilted small talk that ensued. She only knew that somehow, it had. Exiting the now-cold shower, Missy noted that not only did James play havoc with her emotions, he also did nothing for her appetite. Even through the swirling steam, she could make out her protruding collar bones in the vanity mirror.

Sighing, she wrapped her damp hair in a makeshift

turban and knotted a towel around her body. She was reaching for the doorknob when she heard it. It sounded like wood splintering followed by a thud followed by nothing.

Dead silence.

Frozen in mid-reach, Missy prayed she might have imagined it, but knew she hadn't. Her mind, sharp now, explored her limited options. Her phone was in her purse, but her purse was in the kitchen. She kept a bat beside the front door and now she panicked at the thought of a burglar advancing towards her with it in *their* hands.

Silently, she cracked the door half an inch and peeked out. Seeing no one and hearing nothing, she grabbed the only 'weapon' she could find: a pair of manicure scissors. They were a baby step up from the plastic kindergarten variety. Emboldened by the silence, Missy tiptoed from the bathroom and crept along the hall towards her phone.

She was stunned to hear the unmistakable click of her television as it came to life.

Her worst fears were realized. Someone had broken into her home and at that very moment was seated in her living room—watching television!

Chapter 73

"Well, good evenin' doll face! Miss me?"

Luke Weaver, her brutish ex-husband, had crossed a line he'd never before dared to approach. Considering their history, Missy had every right to be terrified, and she was. With his filthy boots propped insolently on her coffee table, he looked agitated and wild-eyed. It was obvious that he hadn't slept in days and was desperate for a fix.

A dangerous combination indeed.

The stink of him added credence to her conclusion. What was left of his hair hung well past his shoulders. To call it unkempt and greasy would be paying it a compliment. Incredibly, his once-washboard belly was even more bloated than the last time she saw it. If he were a woman, one would swear it was triplets!

Luke cackled as he waved what looked to be a check in the air.

"Lookie here what I found in yer mailbox, baby. Twenty-five G's! A shitload of cash fer a little twat such as yerself! Ya must be fucking the hell out of Mis-ter J. Colton, huh? I'm thinkin' that if it's worth twenty-five grand to Mister J. Colton, it's time fer ole Luke to find out what new tricks ya been learnin.'"

Rocking his considerable weight over to one buttock, he made a show of tucking the check into his back pocket.

"Ya don't mind givin' ole Luke a little somethin' somethin', do ya baby? Fer old time's sake?

Missy couldn't remember ever being this frightened. Buying time, she began to babble. She knew she must sound like a complete idiot, but she kept at it as she sidled her way over to where she left her purse.

"Luke, what are you doing here? I thought you were staying at your father's? You didn't say anything about stopping by. Christopher will be home any minute..."

Grinning like a loon, Luke pointed to the floor at his feet. Missy's heart sank along with all hope. Her purse was leaning against the sofa directly beneath his legs. A hulking two hundred and thirty plus pounds grunted with exertion. Not without some difficulty, Luke rose to his feet and started towards her. Missy realized that he wasn't just crazy, he was completely blotto as well.

"Is this what yer lookin' for, bitch? Slurring, Luke shoved her, brandishing her wallet in one hand, phone in the other. She was effectively trapped in her own home. Trapped by the man she'd sworn out complaints against not once, but twice. Missy was positive she was about to become just another domestic violence statistic.

Luke shoved her again. She hadn't regained her balance from his first assault, and now, she couldn't maintain it at all. She went down hard, knocking the breath from her lungs and the useless mani-scissors from her hand. The towel that once defended her modesty was now a useless pile of damp cloth just beyond her reach.

"Yer lookin' mighty tasty these days, bitch..."

She felt the bile rise in her throat when Luke fell heavily to his knees and began to crawl up on top of her. His words rang in her ears.

Finally, blessedly, she lost consciousness...

Chapter 74

James saw the broken lock and unhinged door and was horrified. Gone was the fatigue that dogged him since the adrenaline high turned bad. If anything happened to Missy, he would not be able to live with himself. Especially when he knew months ago that the flimsy lock was as good as useless. More decorative than protective, he despised himself for doing nothing about it.

Missy...

James served two tours of duty during Desert Storm. That was decades ago now. Yet, in the blink of an eye he was back in full combat stance, six senses on high alert. Prepared for anything and everything, he climbed the front steps and entered the house without a single floor-board creaking.

The scene that greeted him was nothing like Kuwait but was fraught with danger nonetheless. James took in the big picture and the minutest detail at the same time. He calculated how to best defuse the situation while multiplying the odds of Missy coming out unscathed.

Little one...

She was nude and just regaining consciousness. She was doing her best to wriggle out from under the huge man astride her. *Her best effort wouldn't be nearly good enough!*

He watched as the man hefted his belly in order to unbuckle his belt and unzip his pants. James was thankful for his timing, if nothing else. He listened to Missy's heart rending pleas for mercy and for the drunken beast to come to his senses. She called him Luke and begged him to think of his son.

James knew everything he needed to know, and quickly

formulated a strategy. Terrorizing the fairer sex was scraping the bottom of the barrel in his book. Men were meant to protect and provide, a detail this gelatinous waste of skin chose to disregard.

Luke, and those of his ilk, gave real men a bad name. It was pathetically clear that he hadn't assumed one iota of accountability in his entire life. Not for his wife and not for his child. And, certainly, not for himself. Instead, he chose the persona of a drunken, misogynistic bully—effectively relieving himself of a real man's culpability.

James had to admit that the role suited Luke to a T. Grubby and obese, the stench of stale wine and body odor emanated from his every pore. The once white undershirt that he sported was a filthy shade of gray and at least two sizes too small. James never understood where the term 'wife-beater' originated. He did now.

My precious...

To Missy, sprawled terrified and naked on the floor, Luke must look like her worst nightmare. To James, he was simply an irritating gnat that needed to be quashed. He knew his type only too well. His voice was low, just loud enough to stop Luke dead in his tracks.

"What do you think you're doing, Lukie boy?"

Luke's head snapped up at the jeering belittlement that seemed to come out of nowhere. His eyes narrowed threateningly, but not before James caught the spark of fear and indecision in them.

"Who the fuck are you?"

James advanced almost imperceptibly. As distraction, he continued to taunt, playing to Luke's alcohol-bloated ego.

"What's the matter Lukie boy? Only the big man when

it comes to beating up women? I'm guessing a hundred and ten pounds is about your limit, then?"

Missy, pinned immobile, began to sob with relief...

Chapter 75

James' arm shot out so fast that Missy wondered if she imagined it. Promptly relieved of Luke's crushing weight, she knew her prayers were answered.

Ironically, James had Luke by the throat and pushed up against a wall. Much the same as he'd done to her once upon a time. She would have swooned at the memory if circumstances were otherwise. As it was, she was happy just to breathe.

While his stance was familiar, his agenda was markedly otherwise. Luke's face was turning a most interesting shade of mottled purple, one that suited him remarkably well in Missy's opinion. When he opened his mouth, she was certain he was about to beg for mercy. The same mercy he'd no intention of showing her. In the end, all that came out was a strangled gurgle.

Eye to eye with Luke, James spoke soothingly to Missy.

"You have nothing more to fear, little one. This pathetic excuse for a man won't be bothering you again."

"Please fetch me a pair of your stockings and call the police. I'll wager they do more than just file the report this time." He leered at Luke and actually chortled, "The third time's gonna be the charm, don't you agree, Lukie boy?"

He was still looking Luke square in the eye.

"Oh, and please cover yourself, pet. This sorry boor wasn't smart enough to appreciate you when he had you. He's seen far more of you than he ever deserved."

For the first time since the nightmare began, Missy realized she was naked. Covering herself as best she could, she scooped up her phone and hurried from the room. She would follow James' directives to the letter.

As she was born to do...

Chapter 76

"And of course, you know better than to bother with bra and panties."

His words caught up with her halfway down the hallway. To her, they were the most beautiful words ever spoken. She giggled imagining her ex-husband's apoplectic face upon hearing them.

After what she'd just been through, giggling wasn't as insane as Missy condemned it to be. Tamping down the euphoria borne of relief, she focused every ounce of her frayed concentration on the task at hand.

Climbing into a short sheath, she called 911. She was relieved to hear that there was a car in the area. It would be there within minutes, possibly seconds. Opening her underwear drawer, she grabbed a pair of panty hose and ran back to the living room. Stockings were a luxury she'd never indulged. Blushing, she handed the nylons to James. As usual, he intuited her very thoughts.

"No stockings, pet?"

He wedged one knee snugly between Luke's thighs, up close and personal to the faux family jewels. Only then did he release the carotid arteries. Tearing the pantyhose in half, he wrapped them around Luke's wrists and ankles and tied them off with intricate knots.

"We shall have to remedy that, won't we? Obstructing access to what is mine is almost as insolent as removing your collar without permission."

Missy couldn't tell whose astonished gasp was louder, hers or Luke's. Pupils dilated, his eyeballs appeared to have vacated their sockets. Clearly, he didn't have a simpleton's clue when best to shut up.

"Wha' the fuck?"

James was silent. Holding onto Luke's arm, he hopped him over to the only chair in the room and, with a shove, 'helped' him to sit. He was ever-so-polite when he asked if she might spare one more pair of hose. Once procured, he proceeded to scrunch them into a tight wad. The entirety was then shoved unceremoniously into Luke's gaping mouth.

There was nothing left to say. At least, not where Luke was concerned. She watched in awe as James smiled into Luke's furious countenance.

"On the other hand, scumbag, panty hose look absolutely *fabulous* on you. Please consider these a gift."

"From Missy…"

Chapter 77

"Speak freely, little one."

And so she did. For the entire time it took to navigate the shortest route between her house and his. Well, almost the entire time.

Whore!

The police had arrived quickly, as promised. Neither officer bothered to hide their snickering at the innovative makeshift gag. Removing it from between Luke's fetid teeth, they turned their attention to the nylon knots at his wrists and ankles. Missy was mystified when their snickering stopped as their jaws proceeded to drop. In unison, they looked first at each other, then at James. There was respect in their eyes.

James smiled enigmatically back, offering his assistance. Missy found herself wanting to take a much closer look at those knots. Unfortunately, any opportunity to do so was dashed when one of the officers produced what looked like a box cutter. The knots were quickly reduced to a pile of unremarkable frayed nylon.

Thus ensued the cuffing of wrists, the reading of rights and the taking of statements. Finally, mercifully, she and James were alone. He sat in the chair vacated by Luke and pulled Missy into his lap. Wrapping her in his arms, he buried his face in her hair. He rocked her as a parent might a frightened child. He held her like a man who had just come *this*close to losing the most precious thing in his life.

Again.

Words were redundant. Silently, they awaited the arrival of the contractor. The door would be secured against intruders for the night. In the morning, it would be replaced.

She was to spend the night with James.

Now, belted securely in the passenger seat beside him, it was her opportunity to speak. At long last, it was her chance to say the words which had echoed a thousand times in her head. She grabbed at it.

Still somewhat dazed and confused, she was determined to leave nothing on the table. There was too much at risk. Missy loved him, it was just that simple. Her words shook with the strength of that emotion. She was so sorry for how she'd behaved, for running away like an immature, spoiled child. She should never have stuck her nose where it had no business.

More than anything, she felt sick to her stomach just thinking of how she'd dispensed of his beautiful collar. She pleaded with James to understand. It meant more than she imagined possible.

Apprehensive, she stretched her little hand across the console. When it was immediately engulfed by his, Missy nearly sobbed. His grip tightened meaningfully with her last words.

"And, sir, I'm so terribly sorry for your loss…"

Chapter 78

"Ah, little one, it's been one hell of a day. I think it's time you stopped talking and started sucking, wouldn't you agree?"

Keeping his eyes on the road, James released her hand. Serenely, he unzipped, pulling his flaccid cock from his pants. Feeling her eyes upon his drooping member, he spoke as if he hadn't heard a single word she said.

She would never guess how tightly his throat was constricted. While he managed to avert tears, James knew there would be no shame in crying in front of this magnificent woman. He glanced over at Missy, smiled magnanimously, and shook his tired cock in her direction.

He may have blown her mind, but her body obeyed flawlessly. James was driving an Audi TT convertible. He was nothing short of amazed at how quickly she managed to spread herself across the tiny car's console and latch onto his cock. With the top down and Missy's ass high in the air, James was almost sorry there weren't more cars on the road to appreciate the splendid view!

There was no wiggle room to speak of, yet Missy managed to take the entirety of him into her warm, wet mouth. With her head in his lap, he spoke as she suckled, motionless.

"I too have much to apologize for, my precious. I demanded much of you, yet offered little in return. There is no excuse for not telling you of Angeline. It pains me that you discovered her in such an appalling manner."

Reaching down with one hand, he stroked her cheek and adjusted her lips on his member.

"I am only human, little one. I allowed my ego to get in the way of my good sense and it almost cost me what I value most in the world – *you!*"

Inserting a finger between her lips to join his cock, James was direct.

"Can you forgive me, pet?"

A verbal response was not forthcoming, for obvious reasons. Nevertheless, James *did* receive a response—and a fervid one at that.

It came by way of Missy's mouth, as it pulled even more ardently at his cock. Her tears of joy soaked clean through the thin material of his slacks.

Submissive…

Chapter 79

"Kneel!"

She stopped dead in her tracks and turned to face him. They were barely ten feet inside his massive front door. Taking her by the elbow, James led her to spot mere inches from the luxurious carpeting of the foyer.

"Kneel, whore!"

She could tell by his curt tone that he was in no mood for vacillation. Eyeing the soft carpet longingly, she knelt on the cold planks of the hardwood floor. She positioned herself as she was instructed months ago. For Missy, the exacting posture was as natural as breathing.

Expecting praise, she looked up. His visage was dark, foreboding. Missy could plainly see the storm approaching. What came was not praise. Not even close.

"Eyes down!"

Bending, James twisted both protruding nipples. He spoke over her anguished yelps of pain and surprise.

"You are kneeling in the exact spot where I found your collar. Apologies are one thing, whore. Disrespect is quite another. You will learn that it will not be tolerated."

Releasing the mashed nipples, he stood. James hadn't bothered to zip up when they'd exited the car. His suddenly titanium-stiff cock leaped out to bob before her eyes. The angry tip leaked a stream of pre-cum, which he cavalierly smeared across her face. He alternated between masturbating one second and availing himself of her wet, accommodating mouth the next.

Missy was either gagging on cock or gasping for air, as James saw fit.

"There will be no collar until you can prove yourself worthy of the honor. I do, however, have a deep desire to mark you in the meantime. Kneel up and smile pretty, little one."

Mouth full, Missy kneeled up without incident. Blushing from head to toe, she somehow contorted her over-stuffed features into a garish smile. Although utterly mortified, her craving for this man continued to escape her body in torrents.

Whore!

There was nothing to be done as it oozed in viscous threads to the floor. James never shifted his gaze from the expanding pool of cunt juice. With little fanfare, he pulled out of her throat and blew an enormous load into her still distorted face.

Wave after wave of ejaculate coated her features. It dripped from her hair and scalded her eyes. It clogged her nostrils and glazed her lips. She moved not a single muscle. James, humming tunelessly, re-inserted his sticky, already deflating cock into her mouth and waited.

With perfect understanding of where she belonged and to whom, Missy lovingly sucked it clean.

Master...

Chapter 80

James lifted her from her knees and into his arms. With his seed congealing on her face, he brought her to his bedroom. Kicking open the door, he carried her meaningfully across the threshold and deposited her onto his king-sized bed. Tenderly, he removed her little dress.

Missy squinted through one cum-swollen lid to see the room where it all began. Turning her head slightly, she saw glimpsed a beautifully framed photo of a woman. Recognizing herself, she burst into tears.

It was taken the day they went for dinner at Dominic's Crab Cave. She had no idea he'd snapped it. She was unable to take her half-eye from it. Missy knew she'd never looked happier.

In a perfect missionary position, James maneuvered his exhausted cock inside of her. While his penis was lifeless, he filled her heart to over flowing. Sharing cold semen between motionless lips, Master and whore found themselves deep within the other.

Sheathed in her grasping cunt for the very first time, Dominant and submissive moaned into the others opened mouth.

As one, they felt their souls entwine.

Missy teetered precariously on the soft edge between slumber and wakefulness. She reveled in the weight of him, snoring softly atop her. She had one last conscious thought before succumbing completely.

She contemplated what might be required in order to merit her collar back. She knew in her heart that whatever the task, she would perform it with the utmost of pride.

He was her Master. She would never doubt him again.

With cum-stained lips curled into a contented half-smile of anticipation, Missy joined James in deep, dreamless sleep...

* * * * *

If you enjoyed MASTERED, please do the author the honor of leaving a short review. Reviews are an indie author's life blood.
If you're dying to know what happens next to Missy and James, TRUSSED, Book 2 in The MASTERED Saga, is available now.
TRUSSED AS GOOD AS MASTERED!
viewBook.at/GETTRUSSED

* * * * *

About the Author

K.L. SILVER writes erotica novels and XXX novellas.
She adds a psychological edge which keeps YOU, the reader, on the edge of your seat. Or, such is the plan.
If that doesn't work, there's also a *ton* of hot S-E-X!
Now, where were we? Oh yes...
K.L. grew up, and still lives on the frozen prairies of central Canada. She lives alone, because she can. Her children have grown up to become strong, independent, and most exciting of all—gainfully employed adults. (YES!)
K.L.'s crazy enough to believe yoga and instant coffee keep her sane. Her primary goal is to write a great story. Her second, of course, is world peace.
Namaste

www.ingramcontent.com/pod-product-compliance
Lightning Source LLC
Chambersburg PA
CBHW051245250626
47155CB00009B/3171